www.tredition.de

AF185141

Alas, the pen is as mighty as the sword: they both wield the power to set free what life and love you may have locked away inside.

B. Hernandez

B. Hernandez

Beaten Dogs

© 2014 B. Hernandez
Umschlag, Illustration: B. Hernandez
Lektorat: Christine Baumgart
Übersetzung: Julia Ritter

Verlag: tredition GmbH, Hamburg

ISBN
Paperback   978-3-7323-2038-7
Hardcover   978-3-7323-2039-4
e-Book   978-3-7323-2040-0

Printed in Germany

1

"Where the hell are we going?"

"Be patient, Alex. It's only a small detour. I need to get a present for my son's birthday. Don't worry, you'll get yours right after."

"Yeah, well, just remember I can't stay away too long. My boss always gives me shit about heading out during lunch hour. It's the busiest time of the day."

"Don't tell me you give a flying fuck what your boss says. Or have you suddenly turned Mr. Career Man on me? Seeing as you've just been promoted from bun warmer to salad-and-onion chopper?"

"Bite me."

"I won't. But you'll bite me, very gently. And soon enough, too, don't you worry."

With a slight shake of his head and a suppressed grin Alex turned away from Nicole and looked out the passenger-side window.

"You really are quite the little bitch."

She took her eyes from the street to cast him a twinkling sideways glance and answered: "And that's exactly what you like about me."

Alex pretended not to have heard. They drove on in silence for a while.

He'd been working at the downtown sandwich joint for almost a year now, serving a clientele of minor clerks from the business high-rises who custom-ordered their sandwiches from the deli counter.

He had started out as bus boy. The deli had a few tables, which were frequented only by old people and students except during peak hours. After a while, they put him on different stations – production, the counter – just like all the other employees.

Nicole was one of the regulars; she came by almost every day, usually buying a small cheese on rye, green salad, and mineral water. You couldn't call that a meal, as she herself freely admitted, but it beat the hunger and didn't ruin her figure. That's how Alex and she started talking. At first it was just the usual banalities exchanged with the customers as their sandwiches were stacked or their purchases rung up. But soon the banalities turned into the kind of banter that evolves almost organically when two people share a wavelength. At some point, Alex noted that she would choose carefully where to stand in line so that she'd get served by him. Sometimes, when she misjudged and was about to be asked by one of his colleagues what she'd like, she would pretend to get a call on her mobile and let the next in line go first. And once, when Nicole finally came in much later than usual and Alex took a break because she was the only customer there and took a seat at her table where she was just about to eat her sandwich and salad, it became almost immediately clear where all this was heading. Nicole finished her meal and took him to a motel room and that was the start of the affair which they had kept going for the past six months or so. They'd meet three or four times each month, either during her lunch break or right after she left her office for the day. They'd screw in her car in some underground parking lot or get a room in some motel near the city limits or went to Alex's small apartment, though they seldom did that. No lengthy talks, no dining or other activities. Actually, they were virtual strangers. All he knew about her was that she worked for some major insurance company and her office was close to his place of work, she was married and had two kids. Plus, she was easy on the eye and willing to fuck him. That anyway was basically all he cared about. The rest wasn't important. She also made it clear from the very beginning what she wanted from him and what she didn't. She was quite the little bitch. And Alex liked that. Sometimes a little more, sometimes a little less.

"I'm working the cash register and the counter. I haven't been in production for ages."

"I know, cutie. I bought my lunch from you just yesterday, remember?" Then she slapped his thigh. "Come on, stop being grouchy. You know it was just a joke. Who cares what job you've got."

Not her, that was for sure. And he didn't usually care either. But sometimes her little jokes were just a bit too bare-knuckled to be funny. There was nothing wrong with bussing tables or chopping onions. It wasn't any less shitty than sitting on your butt behind a desk all day long sorting papers and processing emails and going to boring meetings. At least a sandwich was something useful, something people needed to feel satisfied or, in the case of the office workers, to survive.

Alex had dropped out of college for good in the middle of junior year, having tried several majors, none of which seemed to stick. He worked as an intern in a bank but quit that, too. That was four years ago. Since then he'd been working odd jobs – whatever struck his fancy and only for however long he enjoyed it. You had to make a living and he was determined to earn the money he needed. That was all he wanted from a job. His parents of course saw things quite differently. They felt it was *truly regrettable* that he hadn't *made the most of the great opportunities a college education offered a young man*. But as long as he didn't come to them for money, they let him *do whatever you think will make you happy*. Each of his by now rare visits to his parents sooner or later ended in the same discussion. He hated that. They never got the chance to go to college so now they wanted him to have what they couldn't – even now, after his disastrous failure they were still willing to pay for it. Alex saw the generosity and selflessness in their insistence, but wasn't it his damned business whether or not he wanted to have that great *opportunity*? He just didn't see why you should only find happiness if you took that wonderful opportunity to go to college and spent your time studying stuff that didn't have anything to do with real life. Or, even worse, if you studied stuff that did have lots to do with real life and was therefore tedious and boring. To hell with it. He had spent two years in college and hadn't even known how to properly chop an onion when he started working at the deli.

On the other hand, he had often wished he could swap some of the people he'd worked with for someone with a slightly broader perspective. His current boss was a case in point. He was nothing but the longest-serving member of the sales team, responsible for drawing up the schedule and making sure all the diverse tasks were taken care of. Yet he acted like the sun shone out his ass. And he had the IQ of a stale slice of toast. A very tiresome combination. If you dropped a plate or a slice of meat you'd get penalty points you had to work off during an extra shift cleaning the bathroom or scrubbing the trashcans. He called it *education on the job* or *learning for life*. He himself, he never, not a single time, managed to arrange a work schedule that didn't conflict with anyone's part-time status, off-days, or daycare hours – which, of course, was never his fault. The staff had to arrange their shifts among themselves to keep the store running smoothly. Alex could only tolerate the cretin because he knew he could quit anytime and move on to something else. Maybe he should do that soon. If you looked at it that way, Nicole was right on the mark: his boss was an asshole and Alex didn't give a flying fuck about him.

"So how old is he gonna get?"

"Who? Kenny?"

"If that's what your son is called, yes. Kenny."

"Seven. My husband wanted to get him a game console. I didn't, though. The kids watch enough TV as is, and I wanted to get him something that would make him go outside more. Plus, a dog will help him learn to interact with animals."

"And I guess you got your way."

"Wasn't too difficult. My husband knows what's good for him."

"Oh, I'm sure of that."

She hit his thigh again. This time harder and with her fist.

"Watch it! My husband is lucky to have me."

Alex cried out, rubbed his thigh and twisted his features into an exaggerated mask of pain. "Whatever you say, honey, just don't hit me again."

They both laughed out loud.

"Seriously, though. He agreed pretty quickly, on two conditions: that I be the one to get the dog, and that I get one from the pound."

"Why's that?"

"Because he thinks that after a few weeks the kids will have lost interest and no one will take care of the animal anymore. That's why he wants one from the pound. Easier to return."

"Easier to return? Why bother? Just leave him by the side of the road. With all the dogs just left somewhere, he'll soon find buddies."

"Very funny. We're not that heartless. At least we're giving the little fella a chance for a new home. And if it doesn't work out, well, he'll just go back to the place he knows. No big deal."

"Are you nuts? You can't just push an animal back and forth like that!"

"What are you getting so worked up about? It's just a dog, it won't care who fills up his bowl. And it's not like we're planning to return it right from the start. But if it doesn't work out, it just doesn't. Returning is better than abandoning or even putting it down."

"And when you say that it doesn't work out you mean that your little fella loses interest and won't take care of the dog anymore?"

"'My little fella'? Did you just compare my son to a dog?"

"No. Of course not. All I'm saying is that your husband has a point. Maybe a gaming console is the better birthday present. Little Kenny may not be playing with it forever, but at least you can easily give or throw it away when he's done with it. Besides, dogs tend to pee and poop. And bark. And when you take them out for a walk you need to keep them away from all the other dogs so they won't mate or fight or make mischief. Plus, they have bad breath."

"Hm. Sounds familiar. But after fifteen years of marriage you get used to your spouse's bad breath. And as for you, you always brush your teeth before we see each other."

"Careful. Dogs can bite, too."

"Yes, cutie. But not the ones that bark, right? And why are you so hung up about this? Don't you like dogs in general or do you just want to talk me out of getting one?"

"Phh. I couldn't care less about dogs."

"That's not what it sounded like. Okay, we're here. It's right up there."

Nicole drove into a parking lot and killed the engine.

"It won't be long, I promise."

"Okay. I'll wait in the car."

"Jesus, are you scared of dogs? Come on already. Help me pick one."

With a deep and clearly audible sigh Alex got out of the car and followed Nicole to the animal shelter. He could hear the barking dogs all the way to the parking lot.

The main door led into a wide hallway from which four smaller corridors branched off to each side. The smaller corridors were lined with cages. Each of the cages was like a cube with solid concrete walls on three sides. The fourth side faced the corridor. A mesh door was set in one of the walls. Floor-to-ceiling mesh wire reinforced by steel beams separated the cages from the corridor. Each cage was occupied by three, four, or even five dogs. There were also little doghouses or baskets for the animals to sleep in, bowls, some dog toys as well as pieces of wood and bones for them to chew on. The dogs barked not only at one another but were overexcited because there were other visitors: small kids with their parents, young couples in love, and some elderly people. They all made their way from one cage to the next, stopping in front of a cage, watching, considering, tapping the mesh and iron bars to get the dogs' attention. They all talked to the animals the way they would talk to a baby. Then they moved on. The dogs barked and ran up and down their cages, wagging their tails. Some were shy and didn't come all the way to the mesh where the visitors were standing, others put their front paws up against the mesh and let themselves be petted.

"I'll go and see if I can find one of the keepers, Alex. Why don't you take a look around."

When Nicole returned a little while later with one of the dog shelter staff, a tiny, fragile mildly bored looking elderly man in green rubber boots and green overalls with the shelter's name on the back and his name – Ed – stitched onto the breast pocket, she didn't see Alex right away. She thought he would still be waiting for her near the entrance, since he'd been so reluctant to come in, but now they had to search for him in all the corridors, taking care not to miss him among all the other visitors. Finally they spotted him. He was standing motionless all the way to the back of one of the furthest corridors, looking into the cage there. Nicole looked at Ed, shook her head, and called Alex. When he didn't hear her or chose not to, she and Ed marched toward him. They were alone in this corridor, which was no big surprise as all the cages here were empty. Again she called Alex's name. Only as they came closer did she see, or rather hear, that the cage he was staring at wasn't unoccupied like the others. There was only one dog in the cage, and it barked like crazy. Startled, she stopped in her tracks. She was a few steps away from Alex. He still didn't notice her but watched the dog, calmly. So did Ed. The dog's barks sounded much louder and more aggressive than all the others'. It stood with its head slightly lowered and its legs wide apart, barked at Alex and stopped only to growl and show its teeth. It looked like it would hurl itself against the mesh at any moment and try to tear Alex to pieces. Instead, it suddenly relaxed its aggressive posture and run in circles a few times before starting the whole spiel over again. Finally Ed stepped towards Alex and asked him to move away from the cage so that the dog wouldn't be provoked even more. As soon as the two men moved over to Nicole and out of the dog's sight, there was silence in the cage.

"Found a kindred spirit, did you? I'm ready to go now. I wanted to get a puppy, but they don't have any at the moment. Some adolescents but no baby pups. And I don't want a dog with a past for Kenny. Who knows what these poor devils have been through. Ed says they only give away dogs that have been re-socialized, but I still wouldn't feel good about it. So you men win after all: it'll be the game console. The birthday party's this weekend and I don't have time to check any more dog pounds. It was worth a try, but it wasn't meant to be."

Alex turned towards the cage in the back once more and then looked questioningly at Ed.

"That one came not too long ago. Probably got beaten by the owners. Poor guy. Went almost crazy. Must have been a strong dog, though. Strong and proud. Didn't let them beat the spirit out of him or he wouldn't be so full of life. But even the strongest eventually get lost deep inside and can't find their way again. Most of them get back to being themselves after staying here for a while, when they've had enough time to recover. There must be that click in their heads, then they can go back to normal. It's really amazing sometimes what you can achieve with just a little bit of proper handling. You can make them get used to people again and find them new homes. Most of them, anyway. With that one I'm not sure we can make a change. That dog has gone mean. He might not come back. We'll give him a chance but we might have to put him down. Maybe it's for the best. You can't save all beaten dogs."

In silence the three of them passed the empty cages and went back to the main hallway and the entrance, where Nicole thanked Ed and handed him a tip. Ed opened the door for them, and Nicole and Alex walked to the parking lot. They got into the car and drove back to the city. Alex stared at the street without seeing.

"Jesus, you look like you're ready to jump off a bridge. Did the dogs get to you so badly?"

"The one in the last cage hasn't gone mean. Not yet. But he'll certainly go completely crazy in there, and then they'll have to shoot him."

"How can you know that? Are you the dog whisperer now?"

"He was barking and went into a threatening posture, but in all the time I stood there he never once jumped at the bars."

"So?"

"If he'd really wanted to attack me, the mesh and bars wouldn't have stopped him. He would have blindly followed his instincts."

"If you say so."

"Yes, I do .... I know what I'm talking about. I've seen something like that on TV. The dog was just the same. They had to shoot it at the end."

"Oh Alex, you're really hard to figure out sometimes. Remember what you said when I first asked you to go to bed with me? You said, why not? Everything else is just overrated."

"So? I was right, wasn't I?"

"Yes. But now you're going all mushy about a dog."

"All I said is that the dog isn't mean. But he will go crazy if he stays in that cage."

"So what should they do? Set him free and hope you're right?"

"How would I know? I told you they had to shoot the dog on the TV show. No idea how to do it differently."

"Well, you can't save them all. But you heard the guy: most of the dogs find new homes. Happy end."

"Happy end my ass. Death is the only happy end."

"Please don't share another of your the-world-is-such-a-shitty-place-we'd-all-be-better-off-never-having-been-born moments. They really get me down."

"Okay, okay. No more dog talk. Happy end. Wouldn't want to get you down."

"Don't you start. I'm not the one nearly bursting into tears over some howling dog. You really are unbelievable. On the one hand you're the poster boy for nihilism, someone who doesn't give a shit about the world and life in general. But on the other hand you are compelled in some almost cruel way and in some hidden corner of your soul – or whatever it is you have where others have a soul – to hold on to the pathetic hope that one day, everything will be well and we're all in for a little bit of salvation. It must suck to be you sometimes. And then you get into these horrible moods. Insufferable."

"Yeah, yeah, and you're just a happy ray of sunshine."

"At least I see the bright side of life and know how to have fun."

"By cheating on your husband."

"You know very well what I mean. Or are you trying to get all moral on me?"

"I do know what you mean: your life is so positive and full of fun that you need to cheat on your husband."

"Don't overstep, young man. Or you may find yourself walking back home. What's with the criticizing, anyway? It's not my fault they'll shoot that dog. Or not. Whatever. So get off it."

"Okay, okay. All I'm saying is that you're not exactly the Sunday school role model for moral standards, either. That's why we work so well together."

"What are you talking about? I'm a good person. I'm a religious person. I may only go to church for weddings and funerals, but I do have my faith."

"Fine. But seeing the bright side of life, having fun and a faith don't make you a good person."

"Well, then what does?"

"Cheating on your husband certainly doesn't."

„Come on, I'm not hurting anyone! I'm happily married. I love my husband and children. Sometimes I even love my job. So all in all I'm happy and satisfied with my life. But let me tell you, living such a happy and satisfied life can be hard work. The kids, the husband, the job – as wonderful as it all is, it can be a bit too much sometimes. And sometimes you even get the feeling that you're neglecting your own life, that you're getting lost somewhere in all that. Like losing touch with yourself. And then you wake up one morning and have one of those moments where you ask yourself what you're doing here and what it's all for. You don't want to get up, so instead you turn over and touch the person lying next to you – the one who's been lying there every night for years and will continue to do so for many years to come. He's still sleeping peacefully, blissfully unaware of what's going on inside you. He's just lying there and breathing, sometimes snoring. You look at him, and it feels like it is a stranger laying there, someone who's far, far away from you, someone you hardly know. You try to remember how you love each other, all the beautiful moments you had. And you know that it's true, but you just can't feel it anymore in this very moment. The longer you look at him, the sicker you feel. Those aren't happy moments. And once you have one of them, there'll be others. Yes, I am cheating on my husband. I allow myself to see you. But that's better than swallowing pills or running off. So I don't do it only for myself. And my husband and kids will never know. I'll live with it and I'll die with it. Happy end. Good heavens, we're not living in the darkest Middle Ages anymore. We're only human and we're doing the best we can. That doesn't make us bad creatures, does it?"

"No idea. But you're right though, we don't live in the dark Middle Ages anymore. We're living in the last neon-lit nights of the fun society."

"Mhhm, I like it when you talk all wannabe intellectual, sandwich boy. Turns me on."

"I'm not your fucking sandwich boy."

"Damn right, cutie, you're not. You're my lover boy. And anyway, you shouldn't be casting stones. You're sitting right there in the glasshouse with me. Or tell me, what does your little girlfriend think about our dates? What's her name again? Jessica?"

"Her name is Jasmin."

He wished he hadn't told her Jasmin's real name. When Nicole had told him that all she wanted was an affair, he had assured her she wasn't the only woman in his life, either. It had been a few weeks after he'd met Jasmin. Nicole hadn't asked why he was up for an affair under these circumstances.

She just asked what the other girl's name was. He wished he had lied to her then as he did now whenever they talked about anything but sex and sandwiches. It wouldn't have made what he did any less wrong toward Jasmin. But Nicole belonged to a different compartment of his life. One in which Jasmin shouldn't exist, not even by name.

"So, does Jasmin know about us?"

"No. And she doesn't need to."

"Oh, no?"

"No. I'm not married to her. We're not even exclusive. After all, I haven't known her all that long."

"Uhm."

"What, uhm?"

"Nothing. If you say so. I just wonder what she would say about it. Does she know the two of you are 'not exclusive'?"

Silently Alex looked at her for a moment. Then he turned his head and let his gaze once again get lost on the road that disappeared beneath the car.

It was only through the pull of the safety belt that his attention was brought back to the here and now. Nicole pulled from the main road into a narrow, derelict street and stopped the car.

"Let's be honest Alex, deep inside we both know that salvation is a dangerous pill from the devil's medicine chest and you'll only get it if you go and steal it yourself. Plus, it usually wears off too damn quickly. So come here, my poor little cutie, let me make you forget your pain for one wonderful moment. Come here and fuck me."

2

Alex sat on the stairs in Jasmin's apartment, on the bottom step, tossing his car keys in the air and catching them. He could hear the shouts and laughter of kids playing on the street outside. He heard them so clearly because he had left the front door open. Along with the noise, a balmy late-summer breeze wafted in, announcing a calm, peaceful Saturday afternoon.

"Jasmin! Are you about ready, sunshine?"

Just a minute, Alexander. I think I'll wear the sundress after all. It's still so nice and warm outside."

"Need help getting changed?"

"You would like that, wouldn't you, huh? Fortunately, a lady always knows what's suitable. But if you are nice and behave yourself, you may just help me get undressed tonight. How does that sound?"

"Sounds cruel and like an impossibly long wait."

"Good."

"Good?""

"Well, of course. Women like it when men lust after them. Plus, I enjoy teasing you. Did you put the picnic basket and blanket to the car?"

"Yep, all packed and ready to go. Has been for fifteen minutes now."

He heard the soft, dull steps of her bare feet on the stone steps as she came dancing down.

"Wonderful. Here I am. How do I look?"

"Drop-dead gorgeous."

"You're not mad at me for keeping you waiting, then?"

"No way, sunshine. You're always worth waiting for."

"Thank you. I've been looking forward to spending this day with you, too, Alexander."

"Good."

"Good?"

"Of course. Men like it when women look forward to being with them. Plus, I enjoy teasing you."

"You're incorrigible."

"And you are unbelievable."

She wrapped her arms around him and kissed him. Then she held the embrace for a moment, gazed deeply into his eyes, and finally started smiling softly.

"Is it far to the lake, Alexander?"

"Well, about as far as the last time we went."

"That far, huh? For such a long journey I probably should get changed once more. And you should come and help me so that it doesn't take as long. What do you think?"

"I think you're right; it is one hell of a long drive."

An hour later they headed off to the lake. Alex had opened the top of the old convertible. It was Jasmin's car and she only took it out for special occasions or when the weather was really wonderful. Alex was the only other person she let drive her precious car. No one else, not even her sister or her parents, was allowed behind the wheel. She was very strict about that, because she'd inherited the car from her grandmother, and it meant a lot to her.

The minute Jasmin had her driver's license, her grandmother and her went for drives in the country. The old lady had Jasmin chauffeur her around almost every weekend. The two of them would just drive aimlessly, joyfully, stopping only for a short coffee break. Jasmin sat behind the wheel, Grandma on the passenger side, usually silent, but always smiling. If she did talk, she always told the old stories from her life with Jasmin's grandfather.

Shortly after they got married, the war broke out and Grandpa was drafted. At the beginning, he was stationed nearby so that he could come home most weekends. They hoped and prayed that the war would be over soon, leaving them unharmed. But it wasn't long before the fighting got worse and there seemed to be no end to the war. Grandma lived in constant fear that her husband's unit might be relocated or even moved to the front. This dread soon cast a shadow over all the precious days he spent at home with her. Both found the separation unbearable, yet it was almost as painful to look each other in the eyes and see one's own inner horror mirrored there. The joy of seeing each other these days was always wonderful, but the hours spent together that followed were like an emotional roller coaster ride from the heights of purest, intense love to the deepest, tear-filed sorrow of anticipated separation and death. It was almost too much to bear for their young love.

Then, on one of Grandpa's last days of furlough, after they had "cuddled in bed", as Grandma used to put it, after that wonderful moment together, he stood up and left the house without a word. A few hours later he was back - with a bunch of flowers and the convertible. From then on, they went for drives whenever they were together, as if there was nothing else in the world to worry about. They just drove around, taking only the occasional short break to have a coffee or to cuddle.

Whenever Grandma got to this part of her story, she fought back tears. Grandpa was finally sent to the front and died shortly afterwards. When she learned about his death, Grandma was three months pregnant with Jasmin's mother. Every time she told this story, Grandma emphasized how many wonderful moments she enjoyed with her daughter and her two granddaughters and how thankful she was for it. Yet, she'd say with tears running down her cheeks, nothing compared to the time God gave her with her husband. If you had the chance to experience something that wonderful, a small little death can't destroy it, even though it was extremely hard to bear that Grandpa had to leave so soon.

And now Jasmin had Alex drive her around the country once again. He did not know all the details of the car's history, but he felt proud that Jasmin let him behind the wheel. She hadn't done that all that often. Just sitting in the vintage car had a special appeal to Alex. Mostly, because on the one hand, it made him feel totally at odds – like when everyone they passed would stare and turn their heads as if the car was some kind of alien spaceship. But then on the other hand, he felt absolutely right and at home when he looked at Jasmin sitting beside him, her hair blowing in the wind, a slight smile on her face. Alex watched her, casting her furtive glances when she fell silent or seemed distracted. It was truly amazing: the entire world was the same as it had been all week, and yet it felt completely different today. Being with Jasmin always made the world feel different. A bit strange, actually. But in a very good way.

Suddenly Jasmin cried out and pointed at something at the side of the road.

"There! There!"

"What? Where?"

Alex turned the wheel to get the car back under control, which took him a couple of scary seconds.

She had given him such a fright he almost drove off the road.

"Two little, fluffy bunnies! Sooo cute!"

"What? Two rabbits? Did I hit them?"

"No, no. They were sitting there at the side of the road and ran off when we passed."

"What? That's all? That's why you scream like crazy? You scared me so much I almost drove into the ditch."

"Oh, sorry. Didn't you see them?"

"No, sunshine, I didn't. I'm driving and need to focus on the road."

"But they were sitting right by the road, eating grass. Were you *that* focused?"

"Seems so. I really didn't see them."

"Alexander, don't dream, don't think, just drive and look. I have to keep telling you; otherwise you miss all the good stuff."

"Like a pair of fluffy bunnies?"

"But they were oh, so cute. And looked so funny as they scampered off. One after the other. Totally cute."

"You really fell for them, didn't you."

"Come on, don't be jealous – you're my true cutie."

"Please don't call me cutie … Not right after using the same term to describe a pair of bunnies with their fluffy tails and long ears."

"You're absolutely right. You're not my cutie. You're my Alexander the Great."

"Alexander the Great?"

"Yes! You know Alexander the Great: cunning general, fearless conqueror …"

"You're practically the only person who calls me Alexander. But I'm sure that no one ever called me Alexander the Great!"

When he was a small kid, almost everyone had called him Alexander, the name on his birth certificate. The older he got, the more he became just Alex.

Jasmin watched him as he repeated the name to himself. He bowed his head a little as if he was introducing himself to someone. Then he gave himself an appreciative nod and smiled proudly. When he realized that Jasmin had been watching, he blushed and smiled at his embarrassment. She smiled back and ran her hand through his hair.

The lake wasn't large. It was nestled between the foothills not too near the city and was half surrounded by woods. It was nice and secluded. Along the other half of the lakeshore were some houses and a spacious meadow where visitors could make themselves at home. A few hills, overgrown with high grass, separated the meadow from the edge and the woods. Jasmin and Alex parked the car and headed over to these hills.

Alex flattened the grass so that he could spread the blanket. Jasmin started unpacking their picnic basket, placing the food and dishes on the blanket. He stood watching her for a moment, then he turned to take in the view of the lake.

Alex loved coming here. On bad days, when his job or his life in general threatened to weigh him down, his mind was almost constantly here at the lake. Just the idea of this place helped him relax. He had discovered it on the Sunday walks his parents used to take him on. When he was older, he and his friends used to hang out here after school. And then, for a long time, there had only been him and the lake.

On the other side, where the houses stood, there was an empty plot. It belonged to the family of one of his former classmates. They had lost touch, but Alex had told them that he was interested in purchasing it. One day he would settle here. He could see it now, his house on the lakeshore, two stories, stone walls on the ground floor, dark wood on top, with a balcony and a gabled roof. On the lake side there would be a little terrace, then lawn, all surrounded by a small lattice fence. On his days off, he would set up the barbecue, sit in his deckchair and look out over the lake, waiting for his steak to be done. He saw his children chasing each other all around him, screaming and laughing. A woman – his wife – would come out and bring him a nice, cool drink. She would sit on the chair next to him, and he would know that she was smiling even though he couldn't quite make out her face because the setting sun was in his eyes.

He had a number of different versions of his imaginary life here at the lake. This was his favorite one. The only thing that bothered him was that he could never see the faces of his wife and kids in these daydreams. No matter how hard he tried.

"Alexander, are you going to stand there all day or will you give me a hand"

"Isn't this magnificent?"

"Yes, it is. Would you please put the cold cuts on a plate?"

"Of course."

"How come you know this lake so well?"

"Oh, my parents brought me here when I was a kid. We often came here with the dog."

"You had a dog?"

"A long time ago. I was still a little kid. But I liked playing here with him and hiking around the lake."

"Did he die when you were still small?"

"He was old. Had to go."

"Your parents don't have a dog now, do they? Did you never get another one?"

"No. My father didn't want another one. Not the dog type, you know."

"How is he, anyway? Has he gotten better?"

"You know him. He's back at the bank already, working. Probably still working too hard. And he hasn't given up hunting, either. It must all be a bit too much for his heart, but he won't have it any other way. They don't know how long he has left."

"And how is he dealing with it?"

"He isn't, I suppose. You know what he's like."

"You haven't talked to him, have you?"

"I called my Mother. He wasn't there."

"We should go visit them. I like your parents."

"There isn't a creature on this earth that you don't like, I guess."

"Alexander, don't say that. They're your parents."

"Sorry, sunshine. Won't happen again."

Alex bent down towards Jasmin. As they kissed, he shifted his weight to roll her over on her back, underneath him. He was about to kiss her again when he felt something drop on his leg and foot. It felt like stones falling down on him. Jasmin must have noticed it, too, for she reacted almost simultaneously. She drew up her legs and sat up. A moment later, he heard her laughing. It sounded relieved. A young dog stood smack in the middle of their blanket and was gobbling down the cold cuts Alex had just put on the plate. The mutt must have been drawn by the smell and stumbled over their legs on the way to his prey. Attracted by their laughter and movement, the dog came over to them, but returned his attention to what was left on the plate after sniffing them perfunctorily. Alex tried to push him away from the picnic, but the dog wouldn't budge. Jasmin was still laughing. She held Alex back. Then someone whistled from the edge of the wood. The dog stood motionless and listened, ears pricked. When the whistle sounded again, he snapped up the last bit of meat and ran down the hill toward the wood.

Jasmin and Alex stood and watched him until he reached his owner, who was waiting for him on the path near the edge of the woods. The owner was obviously angry upon seeing that his dog had something in his mouth. He tried to take the piece of meat away from him or at least stop him from eating it. When Jasmin saw that, she ran down the hill towards dog and master. Alex couldn't hear what she was shouting. But her gestures, and the fact that the man let his dog eat his loot, led him to conclude that the little rascal had just gotten away with ten sandwich's worth of premium meat. The man seemed to apologize and took out his wallet, but Jasmin shook her head. They started talking and Jasmin tried petting the dog. The dog did come up to her and let her touch him briefly, but once he noticed that she didn't have any more food on her, he lost interest and disappeared into the woods, nose to the ground. The man followed him, waving Jasmin farewell. No sooner was he gone than they heard another whistle coming from the woods. Jasmin looked after man and dog for a moment, then she danced up the hill towards Alex.

When she was just a few steps away, she stood still and looked at him. She didn't smile, didn't move, just stood there and watched him. The wild grass went up to her knees. A light breeze caressed her sundress and gently tousled her hair. Her face reflected the light of the setting sun. Alex stood motionless on the hilltop. He was paralyzed by seeing her like this.

"Alexander the Great, I really do like you a lot. You are well on your way of becoming my Alexander the Greatest.""

Alex felt all the blood drain from his head. He almost fainted. With an effort he stayed upright on legs that felt suddenly wobbly. As if through a veil, he saw Jasmin taking the last steps toward him at a run.

"Catch me!""

He managed to pull up his arms at the last second. She jumped into them. She had so much momentum that he lost his balance and they both fell, she landing on top of him. She laughed out loud.

"What is it, my strong hero? Don't tell me I'm too heavy for you!""

And they continued where they'd left off when the young dog had disturbed them.

3

Jasmin lay down on the bed next to Alex and rolled on her side, taking care not to wake him. She liked watching him sleep. He was lying on his back, his face turned towards her, his features peaceful. She held still for a few breaths, then she propped herself up on one elbow and bent over him, kissing him softly on his forehead, then his brow, his cheeks, and finally his lips. Alex drowsily opened his eyes. Once he realized what was happening, he returned her kiss. Her hair was wet from the shower and she smelled wonderfully fresh and clean. When he moved his hands along her body, she withdrew.

"Good morning, sleepyhead."

"Hello, sunshine. What a nice way to wake up."

"I'm sure it is. Why don't you keep that in mind in case you should ever be up before me."

"Duly noted. Well, what could we possibly do now that I'm awake?"

"We could put a move on and get to my parents' on time."

"What? I mean, I like your parents, but I could think of several things I'd like even more right now."

"Really? You could think of several things?"

"Well, actually it's one thing. But in many different variations."

"As tempting as that may sound, Alex, we really need to get going."

"Seriously, sunshine?"

"Absolutely. Come on. I'm hungry."

"You know, I think I'm extremely tired all of a sudden. Let's have breakfast in bed and go back to sleep afterwards."

"In your dreams. Come on. Move your cute ass to the shower. My mother's making lunch, and my parents have a strict schedule."

"Your parents don't know that you're coming for lunch. We could go there later, for coffee. That would be way more polite anyway."

"They invited us for lunch."

"They did? So I'm the only one who didn't know that we're supposed to have lunch at your parents?"

"You know now."

"And how long have you known? Did they call this morning?"

"No. They invited us five days ago."

"Well, well, and you only just now thought of telling me? There was absolutely no way you could have let me know before, say, when we spent the whole day together yesterday, at the lake and here at your place? No occasion to mention that lunch date with your folks?"

"I just forgot."

"Of course you did."

"Alexander, you know as well as I do that you very probably wouldn't even have spent the night here if I'd told you before. Or you'd prepare some lame excuse why you couldn't come with me. And I really want you to be with me at my parent's. It's been a while since the last time."

"And now it's too late for my lame excuse, is it?"

"Jesus! If it's such a big deal for you, I'll call and cancel."

"Easy, sunshine, easy. It was just a joke. A stupid joke."

"So we're going?"

"Of course we are. I'm hungry, too. And your mom is a much better cook than you are."

Jasmin laughed, grabbed her pillow and pushed it down onto his face. Alex turned over and lay on top of her, pinning her arms onto the bed. She tried half-heartedly to get free.

"You're a smart cookie, sunshine. You can really read my heart and mind. It's almost a bit scary."

"Nevertheless, you need to hit the shower now."

"I'm so glad the two of you could make it," Jasmin's mother said and gave Alex a big welcoming hug. Then she turned to Jasmin and kissed her on both cheeks. "You're looking good. Unfortunately, your sister can't come today. The twins are sick. We went to visit them yesterday. The poor things really caught a bad case of the flu."

"But they're two strong little troopers, they will be up and running again in no time. Good to see you both!" Jasmin's father had come in from the garden, where he'd been setting the lunch table. "How long has it been since we saw them last? Two or three weeks? It's unbelievable how fast they grow. And they always have stories to tell you, both of them. We would have liked to gather you all, but it would have been irresponsible to make them come. Next time, though! I'm sure by then those boys will be tall enough to storm around the house.""

Jasmin gave her father a hug; then she bumped Alex with her hips. "Wonderful. That means that

Alex will finally be able to play soccer or something with them."

They sat down to lunch, which as always, soon turned into quite an entertaining production. Either Jasmin's mother would jump up because she forgot something in the kitchen, or her father would go get the photo album of the twins, or Jasmin couldn't wait to see the new carpets in the bedroom, or someone spilled something and everybody tried to wipe it up at once, or Jasmin's mother would get more beers for Alex and her husband. In the midst of all that, Jasmin's father served one course after another and put second helpings on any plate that looked empty until finally Alex had to excuse himself to go to the bathroom. When he returned, Jasmin was telling her parents about their trip to the lake the day before. As she got to the part about the dog, she had to laugh so hard she almost choked on her sip of water and nearly spluttered all over the table. Alex had to smile too and clapped her on her back, more to comfort than to help.

"Why did we never have a dog?" Jasmin asked after she finished her story.

"My goodness, child," her mother laughed, "the house was full enough with you and your sister, and you kept your father and me quite busy. I don't think we would have had room for a dog."

"Absolutely", Jasmin's father said. "And if we had wanted another child, we would have asked the stork to deliver it.""

"But still, a dog would have been nice to play and run around with," Jasmin insisted.

"You didn't need a dog for that. Believe me, you did more than your fair share of running around. And there were always plenty of other kids in the neighborhood the two of you could play with," her mother replied.

Her father had turned thoughtful: "We did consider getting a dog when you left home."

"But not for long and never seriously," her mother added with a smile and started clearing the table.

"No, not seriously," Jasmin's father agreed. "When you and your sister moved out, we worried for a while that the house might feel too big and empty. But then, rather quite soon, we realized that we liked having the place all to ourselves. Of course we miss you and think of you every day. Most importantly, we always enjoy having you visit. At first, we couldn't even remember being by ourselves, just the two of us. But let me tell you, your mother and I rediscovered some wonderful, long-forgotten parts of each other. And we're enjoying them even more than we did before."

"Okay, that's quite enough info, Dad," Jasmin said as she got up to help her mother. "There'll be no dog in our family, I get it. And I'll get over it, too. After all, I sometimes take care of my neighbors' dog when they're on holiday and can't take him. I go for walks with him. That'll have to do."

When mother and daughter had left for the kitchen, Jasmin's father turned to Alex: „So, Alexander, did you take the convertible to the lake yesterday?"

Alex nodded.

"Did she let you drive?"

"Yes, she did. Quite an exception, I hear."

"No, no. You driving is not an exception. She's just very particular about that car. Not everyone is allowed to drive it. If she lets you behind the wheel, it means you're special to her and she wants you to drive."

Alex nodded again, blushing slightly. He imploringly hoped that this would be the end of this discussion, or at least either Jasmin or her mother would reappear from the kitchen. As Jasmin's father stood to clear the remaining dishes from the table, he followed suit, relieved.

After they did the dishes together, Jasmin suggested they go for a little walk.

"That's a wonderful idea," her mother seconded. "The fresh air might even make Alexander a little more talkative."

Jasmin grinned challengingly at Alex. "It's amazing, actually – he usually isn't this quiet. Makes for a nice change, though."

"Well, I only talk when I have something to say," Alex replied. When he noticed that his tone was a bit more caustic than he'd intended, he rolled his eyes, gave her a crooked smile and shook his head to make clear that he'd meant it as sarcasm. "It was just interesting to listen to you all. I enjoyed the conversation even without adding much."

They headed out for a leisurely walk around the neighborhood.

"Do you at least talk a little to the Lord?" Jasmin's mother asked him.

For a moment, Alex looked like he'd been slapped. "Talk to the Lord?"

"Yes. You know,to our Lord."

Jasmin and her father fell a few paces behind them.

Alex regained his composure. "Hm, no, I rarely talk to him. I don't think I'm one of those people he really wants to talk to, either."

"Oh, don't you worry about that. There's nobody He doesn't want to talk to. And He also likes to listen. He is Love and he wants to share it with us."

"Okay, then. I guess I will take some time to talk to him when the opportunity comes up."

"Alexander, I know all this sounds a little weird and old-fashioned to you young people. And I don't want to talk you into anything. But it would be very sad if you closed your eyes and your heart and just turned away without having made absolutely certain that there is nothing there for you to see."

Alex turned around discreetly to Jasmin. She reacted immediately and came up to her mother, starting a conversation about the old neighborhood they were walking in. Alex slowed his gait until he walked beside Jasmin's father. The two men let the distance to the women grow larger.

"I have to admit that my talks with the Lord aren't as deep and wide as my wife's either. I went to church this morning, though. We go almost every Sunday. I go because she goes and it means a lot to her. I think she resembles her mother in this respect. What I really mean to say, Alexander, is that I know what I feel for this woman. And it doesn't matter in the end whether you want to call it 'love' in the most magical of sense or just, what do I know, 'apple-cinnamon sauce.' Nor do I give a hoot whether it's just a biochemical reaction or the act of a higher power that I feel this way. None of that changes anything about how I *feel* for her. My wife firmly believes that we enjoy the privilege of experiencing the magical kind of love a benevolent, superhuman entity has bestowed on us. She is a very sharp and intelligent woman. Maybe much smarter, and certainly a lot more reasonable than I am. I don't know, but perhaps that is exactly why she is so convinced that there is a higher power and a magical kind of love. As for myself, if I now have to choose to live in a world in which real goodness may exists or in one, that is totally stripped of any magic whatsoever, I rather choose the former. Anyone with even half a brain would, don't you think? Especially if all it takes him is a weekly trip to church with his beloved wife and an open mind for what might be possible and real."

"Whatever you say. To each his own."

"That's a given. But you can be honest here. This is supposed to be a conversation, not a confession or a test."

"Hm. I don't spend a lot of time thinking about these things."

"Come on, Alexander, now you're just playing dumb. Still waters run deep, as they say. At least that's what Jasmin says about you."

"Does she now?"

"Yes. She is pretty taken with you. But if you don't want to talk, you don't want to talk. That's fine, too."

"I just don't want to hurt anyone's feelings. That's all."

"If you think it hurts my feelings if you have a different view of things, you couldn't be more wrong. If , however, you were to make fun of what I just told you and disrespect me, well, yeah, I'd be hurt. But I don't think you would do that. Right?"

"No, of course not."

"Well then. Speak your mind."

They kept walking for a few steps. Then Alex took a deep breath and exhaled.

"With all due respect to your romantic concept, I cannot warm towards the idea that there is a higher power."

"Because …?"

"Because there's too much shit going on down here. And much of it in the name of some kind of higher power."

"And by 'shit' you mean war, poverty, misery, hunger and all that."

"Not just that. You don't have to look all that far to seriously question the idea of 'our Lord above us.' Our value systems and the way we treat each other can't possibly be of divine nature. Ideas of dignities are all too often used or abused to excuse or justify behavior we know isn't right. Belief systems are just smokescreens to alleviate our conscience."

"Agreed. But isn't that a different question? The question of what we humans try to turn these potential higher powers into?"

"If there isn't one, you can't turn it into anything."

"Exactly. The problem is, however, that we can't be really sure whether or not there is such a thing. And still we try to turn it into a hell of a lot."

"Yes, right. But if it became clear to everyone that all the evidence points against the existence of a higher power, and if everyone acted accordingly, we wouldn't have all those problems. "

"Evidence, right. Let's postpone judgment for now on what it points to. Whether or not a higher power exists isn't even the point. There is no, and might never be a, scientific way to decide that. The fact remains that a majority of the earth's human population is still trying to make something of it. It's a human trait."

"That doesn't make the higher power more real or human behavior more excusable. "

"But it also means that one should ask what we humans make of the higher power and not whether it exists at all. You don't have to strip the whole world of all magic. You just have to look for the human aspects."

"Maybe. But whether or not there is something greater than us – humankind is evil."

"Come on, that's a little hard, don't you think?"

"Everything going wrong on this still-blue planet is on us. Politics, art, science and society reflect exactly what humans are. And they don't look too good right now. Our attitude of 'every man for himself and the biggest piece of the cake for me whatever the cost' is starting to backfire royally. We're the dregs of creation."

"Don't forget that daily life underwent tremendous changes in years past. As the digital world grew, the real world shrank. Maybe what we're currently experiencing is just the impact of this development that is a personal overload for every individual."

"Babylon, Ancient Greece, the Roman Empire – all high cultures declined at some point. Maybe it's time for us to move to the side and let a new one enjoy the spot in the sun. Preferably a whole new species."

"Sure, times are constantly a-changing and so are cultures and societies. They always did. That's a good thing. It means that things keep evolving."

"Only question is, where does this evolution lead us."

"Humankind is still young. I believe too, that there's still a lot we need to learn. But we are learning. Just look at the last few centuries. We didn't do too badly there: we more or less outgrew our adolescence of violent conquest and expansion, we're about to overcome the youthful cockiness of industrialization and are getting a grip on the *'Sturm und Drang'* of the digital age. And I even believe that there are already some small, hidden seeds of the understanding of an adult comprehension in ecological and ethical sustainability sprouting. Excuse the metaphoric embroidering, Alexander, but I think it's fascinating to be human and part of humanity."

"And therefore partly responsible for everything that's going down."

"Oh, no. I'm absolutely not with you on that. Yes, I am part of humanity. Yes, I am doing my part to develop it in a certain direction. But I am not responsible for the whole of humankind and their acts against each other and the planet. It's just like in business: your task, your competence and your area of responsibility need to match or something like that, right? "

"And you don't think it's your task to advance humankind?"

"Well, yes, but only in my area of competence. And therefore only within this limited area of responsibility. Even though 'only' is an understatement. If we all took on our responsibilities, we'd be quite a few steps more advanced."

"What and how large is your area of competence?"

"My area of competence, and therefore of my responsibility, is my own life and behavior. And by 'life' I especially mean everything I pass on to other people. Namely, my children."

"One could say that it is unfair and an imposition to bring children into this world. Unfair for the children, I mean."

"Being born is never an imposition. Being born is always an imposition. It's very hard to have a debate on this, almost impossible. It's like two sides of one coin. But if you really want to make humankind better, you need to influence humankind. You can do that through the way you act. And you can do it even more effectively through your own children. The things you teach them or don't, the way they approach life and the world will change humankind more than anything else ever could. Your children will do the same with their children and so on."

"What kind of thrilling topic are the two of you so immersed in?" Jasmin asked. She and her mother had stopped walking and were waiting for the men to catch up.

"Children," her father answered grinning.

Clearly surprised, both women stared at Alex, who almost took a step back. "What? Children. That's right."

"And what exactly did you say about children?" Jasmin asked with unveiled curiosity.

"Why don't we go through the park and back home. I'm hungry for some cake now," her father deflected.

"I baked one especially for you," her mother added.

But Jasmin had put her arm through Alex's and wouldn't budge: "So what was it about children, huh?"

"Nothing really. Your father only explained that children are our future."

And then, after a moment: "The future of humankind. Children are the future of humankind."

Jasmin's father stepped in: "We talked about how to help modern humankind develop in the right direction. One idea was that one should prepare one's children for life so that they, and the following generations, are able to choose and follow, amongst many, the best possible development for the whole of humankind."

"Like you did with us," Jasmin said, and her parents smiled proudly. "But," Jasmin went on, "knowing Alexander, I bet he didn't want to wait that long and have the whole world saved right away on his own."

"Which is a very honorable aspiration," her father stated.

"Yeah, yeah, just like a hero in the movies." Jasmin shook her head and kissed Alex on his cheek. "All fine with me, as long as he is my hero."

"In the real world, unlike in the movies," her father said, taking his wife into his arms, "one man can almost never change the world. Life is much bigger than any one of us. This powerlessness of the individual is as wonderful as it is cruel. I believe that we have to accept it or it will destroy us. And maybe it even helps us to experience ourselves as worthwhile and appreciated parts of something larger, something that exists above and beyond all of us, rather than having to live with the feeling that we are just powerless victims of random chance."

"Plus," Jasmin added as she laid her head on Alex's shoulder, "there is a lot that we can do and change in our own little worlds. How about a little Lisa and a little Michael?"

Feeling Alex tense up, she continued: "Jennifer and Daniel?"

Alex disentangled his arms from hers and gave her a large-eyed stare. She couldn't hold his gaze without breaking into laughter: "You should see your face right now, Alexander. Calm down. We're not in children territory yet. First we'll have coffee and cake."

But she protracted his torture by calling out new baby names for the remainder of the walk, assisted willingly by both her parents.

Back in the garden, Jasmin's parents served coffee and cake and, mostly for Alex's benefits, numerous memories of Sunday afternoons filled with family games. All the anecdotes and stories awakened a clear yearning for board games. Jasmin took Alex to the big wooden closet where her parents kept all the games. The closet doors opened to reveal stacks and stacks of board game boxes, and Jasmin told him to pick one. Except for 'Memory', the only one that you could play by yourself, he didn't know a single one of them. Finally, he just grabbed one blindly and brought it out to the garden. Jasmin immediately started setting up the board in the middle of the table. Her parents moved the plates and cups aside to make space for rolling the dice. Alex took another piece of cake and announced that he would sit the first round out and just watch to learn the ropes. He resisted the others' assurances that jumping right in was the best way to learn. When the round took longer than he needed to finish his cake, he asked whether it would be okay for him to go inside and watch the football game. He then spent the rest of the afternoon in front of the television. Now and then he could hear excited voices and explosive laughter from the garden.

By the time Alex and Jasmin started home it had become dark. Jasmin looked at him. Whenever they met an oncoming car, his face was lit up for a moment by the headlights before it disappeared again in the half dark of the cabin.

"You look sad. Was today bad for you?"

"I'm just tired, sunshine."

"Really? When my sister is there with the twins, it gets even more exhausting."

"When they are there, I watch sports with her husband the whole time. He never gets to do that otherwise."

"Yeah. The two of you usually stay glued to the box. Too much family intensity for you today, huh?"

"It was … different."

"Different good or different bad?"

"Neither, both, can't say. Just different."

"Yeah, but was in different in a negative or positive way. Come on, what does your gut say?"

"That I had too much cake?"

"Alexander!"

"It wasn't bad. That's for sure. Your parents are just very different from mine. Just different."

"Oh, great idea! Let's go see your parents next Sunday to even things out. I'm sure they'd be happy. Especially now that your dad isn't doing so well."

Alex was silent for a moment. "We'll see. I might have to work next weekend."

"Really? Or is this already the seed for a lame excuse?"

"It's not like visiting my parents is the highlight of our week, you know that."

"Come on, Alexander, don't be like that. I enjoy spending time with you parents."

"Oh? What did you enjoy most last time? My father's monologues about the latest stock analyses and hunting? My mother's top ten reasons why women like her still earn less than men at the same executive level? Or the wonderful silence in between?"

"Don't exaggerate. It wasn't all that bad. We also talked about holiday plans and fashion. Plus, I think it's great that they both are still so interested in their jobs, that they enjoy their jobs."

"Those aren't just jobs to them. They're their whole lives."

They had reached Jasmin's building. Alex stopped the car.

"Whatever you say. Let me know your decision in the next days, Alexander."

"Will do."

"Are you coming in? Will you stay the night?"

"I'd like to. But I have to get up early tomorrow so I better sleep at my place."

"You can get up early here, too. In fact, I also have an early start."

"It's easier this way."

"Are you sure, Alexander?"

Alex bent over toward Jasmin and planted a kiss on her lips.

"I'll think of you before I fall asleep and then I'll dream of you, sunshine."

"You wouldn't have to if you stayed here."

"But this way I'll look forward even more to seeing you again."

"You were wrong this morning. All too often I can't read you at all. But I'm working on it."

"Maybe there's nothing written there."

"Good night, Alexander. Thank you for a lovely weekend."

"I thank you. Sleep tight, dream sweet, sunshine."

4

Alex climbed out of bed and started to get dressed. Behind him, Nicole switched on the little TV mounted on the opposing wall. She was naked on the bed, unwrapping the sandwich and salad Alex had brought with him. The tiny motel room smelled of mothballs and old cigarette smoke.

It was Thursday, just past noon. He hadn't met Jasmin since the last weekend when they went to her parents'. Nor had Alex contacted her a since they had said their goodbyes on Sunday night.

"Are you in a hurry, Alex? The room is paid for. We can stay all night."

"I have to get back to work."

"Come back to bed. Consider it customer service. You don't want to lose one of your regulars, do you?"

"Was the service not to your liking, then?"

"Oh, the service was fine. But I never said that I had enough."

Alex sat down on the bed, resting his back against the headboard and looking at the TV.

"How was your kid's birthday party?", he asked.

"Not that again. Do you want to spoil my lunch?"

"Just wanted to know if he enjoyed the console."

"He's enjoying it tremendously. My husband and I, we hardly get to see him anymore."

"Well, I guess it's a good thing then that you didn't get him a dog."

"And how was your weekend? Spent it with Jessica, did you?"

"Jasmin. Her name is Jasmin. And yes, I did."

"Did you do anything or did you just stay in bed?"

"Very funny."

"What? Isn't she as good as me?"

"We went to see her parents."

"Well, well. And? How was it?"

"Jasmin's mom made lunch. It was good."

"I wasn't talking about the food. Is her mom a bad mother like me?"

"Hardly", Alex murmered.

"Ouch. But don't you forget, cutie: you're the one fucking me."

"I guess her parents are alright."

"You guess they're alright? This sandwich here is alright. Is that all you can say about her parents? You people did talk, didn't you?"

"Yeah, sure, but I didn't pay that much attention. We had lunch and then I watched TV. The game was on."

"Showed them your very best you, huh? And do they still like you?"

"Don't know."

"Come on. Did they give you the evil eye or were they nice to you."

"Everyone's nice to their guests."

"So, they do like you. And that makes you feel awkward. You are a strange man, Alex."

"Don't forget that you're the one letting me fuck her."

"Well, maybe I like strange."

Nicole offered Alex the uneaten half of her sandwich. When he declined, she wrapped it in a napkin and started poking around in her salad. He watched her absent-mindedly for a moment.

Then Alex suddenly asked: "Say, do you think that we are evolving?"

"You and me?"

"You, me, the whole of humanity."

"Where's that coming from all of a sudden? Your associative leaps are truly astounding."

"Just trying to start a little lunch conversation. Never mind, I'll watch TV."

"Easy, boy. What do you mean by 'evolving'?"

"You know. Learn new things. Spiritual and psychological growth and all that. Get better at dealing with one another and the world."

"Sure, we are always changing. Everything always changes with time, right? We become different. But not better. What does 'better' mean, anyway. Better, worse – those don't really exist, Alex."

"Do you mean different as in more mature, wiser … happier?"

"There you go again on your search for paradise. Why can't you just *Be* and enjoy what there is, what we have? Look around: everything's great. We're having fun. And compared to the vast majority of mankind we're living a pretty damn good life."

"Shouldn't everyone live a pretty good life, Nicole?"

"No one ever said that life was fair. That's just another reason to just be happy, don't you see?"

"And how do you know that our lives are 'good'? Just before you didn't even know what 'better' meant."

"Alex, what is it you want to hear? What do you want me to say? What will shut you up? One fine day, the angels will come down from heaven, make all the bad stuff go away, and we'll all live happily ever after in the Garden of Eden like a big family?"

"Don't be stupid. That's not what I was talking about."

"So what were you talking about, Alex?"

"I don't have the right words for it. Maybe something like soul growth – a little more love and empathy and responsibility for each other and life in general."

"As I said: angels from heaven."

"No, not at all. You always have to ridicule everything."

"You think I'm ridiculous? Did they recite *Hamlet* to you at her parents' house or what? Horatio, the world is what it is. And life is what you make it."

"Well, maybe. Perhaps you're right."

"Guess that's why I like you so much – you're a dreamer. A totally hopeless and lost cause."

"So you don't want to save me?"

"Cutie, I'm not Jasmin."

"This has nothing to do with her."

"Whatever you say. Just be honest with yourself. You'll see I'm absolutely right."

"What do you mean?""

"Wherever your dreams may usually take you, Alex, in real life, here and now, you're with me anyway."

Alex stared fixedly at the TV. Nicole finished her salad, got up, and tossed the empty plastic container and the napkin with the sandwich into the trash can. She glanced out the window and stretched. When she got back into bed, she grabbed the remote control and turned off the TV. Then she started snuggling up to Alex. She pushed one leg over his and turned over until she came to sit on his lap, facing him. With her knees on both sides of his hips she arched her back and threw her head back. When Alex didn't respond, she took hold of his right hand, moving it up along her body, between her breasts, to her lips. She placed tender kisses on his palm and started caressing it with the tip of her tongue. Then she placed his middle fingers in her mouth, sucking on it from root to tip. She moved his wet finger down her body and inserted it into herself.

"You like that, don't you, Alex? Your very own little piece of paradise."

Alex pulled back his hand.

"I really should get back to work now."

Nicole glared at him. When Alex didn't flinch, she climbed off him and moved over to the empty side of the bed.

"Then buzz off, sandwich boy."

He stood up and moved over to the door.

"You know Alex, things have become quite tiresome lately. I might start looking for someone else if you keep on like this."

He stopped and turned around. Their eyes met.

"That may be for the best, Nicole."

"What's that supposed to mean? Is this it?"

He seemed to hesitate a moment. Then he said:

"Yes, this is it."

"Because of her? For her? Do you think this will change anything? Do you believe you will change? Come on Alex, grow up. Stop dreaming."

"Well, at least I still know how to dream."

"Pfff. You'll make the poor girl unhappy."

Alex looked at Nicole silently, then left the room and went back to work.

Jasmin had tried to call him several times during the past week, but he'd just let it ring. He didn't feel like talking to her or even seeing her. The whole week he'd been feeling tired and sluggish. He slept fitfully. His mind and soul seemed to be dimmed as if packed in cotton. The only good thing about this lethargic torpor was that it enabled him to switch to autopilot at work and inoculated him against any unpleasantries there.

Even his breakup with Nicole left him largely unaffected this afternoon. It had been an unsavory moment, but it hadn't touched him deeply. Instead, his thoughts kept going back to Jasmin – and even more so since his lunch encounter with Nicole. Before his shift was over this afternoon, he dropped first one, then another sandwich he was preparing. He had never been clumsy at work before. It was more than clear that Jasmin would be mad at him for not calling or dropping by all those days. They'd been through it before. Usually, he would just come by at her place when he felt like meeting her again and mumble some excuse about having been terribly busy or something. Jasmin would scold him a little and act mad for a while, but her anger would evaporate soon and they'd make up. This time, he felt none of that playful casualness. Several times he even thought about calling her to ask if it was okay for him to come by this evening. Or at least ask how she was. The more he thought about it, the more ridiculous he felt. And the more he yearned to see Jasmin.

Late that evening, Alex drove by Jasmin's building. There was light in her window. She was home. Slowly, Alex turned the corner and circled her block. When he came round her corner once again, he checked that her light was still on. Again, he passed her driveway and drove on. After a few hundred yards, he turned and parked at the curb. He killed the engine but didn't get out of the car. He just sat there, watching his fingers drumming a beat on the steering wheel, as if that inane rhythm was an excuse not to get out of the car. It almost sounded like heavy raindrops drumming on the roof in a thunderstorm. Finally he stopped, threw himself back in his seat, crossed his arms to keep his hands in check, and took a few deep breaths. He could smell the fresh scent of the flowers on the passenger seat. They were Jasmin's favorites. He grabbed them and got out of the car. He took a few steps toward her place, then stopped. He looked at the flowers. Of course they would make her happy. Not just because he remembered her favorite flowers but because he finally also thought of bringing her some. She would want to know why he brought them. Why today, of all days. He didn't know how to answer that. In fact, he didn't know what to say to her at all. The only thing he knew was that he wanted to see her and be with her. He went back to the car and put the flowers on the passenger seat. Then he walked over to her building and rang the bell.

"Well, well, if it isn't Alexander the Great honoring the ordinary womenfolk with his royal presence."

She left him standing in the doorway and returned to her living room. Alex followed her.

"Hello, Jasmin. I'm sorry. This is the earliest I could make it."

"Really? Someone got sick at work again so you had to take over the shifts?"

"No. I just … I couldn't make it any earlier."

"You just couldn't? You *just* didn't get the chance to pick up a phone and call?"

He went over to the couch and sat down. She remained where she was, standing in the middle of the room, arms crossed, and watching him closely.

"Jasmin, please. Let it go. Just this one more time. I promise it won't happen again. And you're not 'ordinary womenfolk'. To me you are extraordinary."

"Nice try. But you won't get away that easy. Four days, Alexander! I haven't seen or heard from you for four long days!"

"I really missed you. You have to believe me."

"Excuse me? You can't be serious, can you? Missed me, huh? Well, evidently not even enough to call. Do you think I'm brainless?""

"No, I don't."

"But?"

"Nothing. I just couldn't get in touch. I had to … figure out a couple of things."

"What things?"

"Maybe it was less that I had to figure them out. They had to become clear."

"What things?"

"You. Me. Things."

"How do you expect anything to become clear if you don't even know what it is you need to become clear? If this little act here is all you got, you shouldn't have come here, really. Maybe that's what you had to get clear."

Alex got up and stood by the window near the couch. He looked down on the street. Dusk had turned to darkness. He moved both hands through his hair and folded his fingers behind his head. For a long moment he kept still; then he let his arms drop to his sides and turned around. Jasmin had sat down on one of the chairs at the dining table across the room.

"Jasmin, I really like you very much."

"Thanks a lot."

"I mean it. Whenever I'm with you I feel like I'm in another world. One I would like to get to know and see more of."

"How nice for you. And this is how you thank me? By making me unhappy?"

Alex winced inside. Shaken, he paused and looked at Jasmin. She was sitting calmly at the table, seeming to wait for his reply.

"I make you unhappy?"

"When you behave like you did this past week you make me a little unhappy, yes."

His gaze was still fixed on her, but it went right through her to nowhere. As if struck by a sudden inertia, he slumped down and sat on the windowsill behind him.

"I make you unhappy," he murmured.

Jasmin pushed back her chair and walked over to him. Alex lowered his head. She stopped one step away from him.

"Listen, Alexander, I'm not mad at you anymore. But please don't do this to me ever again. If you really like me it's time you started behaving accordingly."

He lifted his head and looked at her. His eyes were brimming with tears.

"I'll make you unhappy," he whispered, his voice faltering.

Jasmin shook her head.

"What are you talking about? What is it with you today? You're acting strange."

She stretched out her hand to caress his cheek. But Alex turned away from her, evading her touch. Startled, Jasmin pulled her hand back immediately. She looked at him, horrified. Under her gaze Alex felt even more weighed down. He could hardly breathe. A white-hot wave of panic rose up from deep inside him and drove the blood into his head. His vision got blurred, his ears felt muffled, and his thoughts seemed to explode in all directions. He needed to scream for help: "I'm having an affair."

For what felt like an eternity, everything froze. Both of them even stopped breathing. Then a wavering smile broke through Jasmin's mask of a face.

"You're kidding, right?"

Alex hid his face in his hands. Jasmin turned away and took a few steps back. Her breaths came in a violent staccato, and she fought with everything she got against the storm rising in her – a storm that threatened to take all her senses. She tried to take several heaving breaths. She wanted to speak, but her voice wouldn't get through the knot in her neck, so all that came out were sobs. She put a hand on her mouth to quiet herself, but to no avail. Tears started rolling down her cheeks. Behind her, Alex had gotten up and moved toward her. When Jasmin noticed, she flinched and held up a hand to stop him. He sat back down on the couch and stared into empty space. Several minutes passed. Jasmin collapsed on the dining chair. Now and then he could hear her blowing her nose. After a while there was silence. Alex waited, motionless. He did not know what to do. The silence felt strangely comforting. If it weren't for the light in the room, he would have felt completely invisible. Over at the table, Jasmin took several deep breaths.

"Is it me? Do you think it's all going too fast?"

As if that was the cue he'd been waiting for, Alex jumped from the couch. He started towards her but then stopped in his tracks. His heart was pounding.

"Jasmin! For sure it's not you! It's me. It's all my fault. I made a big, a horribly big mistake. I don't know ..." But he could not continue. He was choked up with tears.

"Tell me why, then. Just tell me why!"

But Alex couldn't talk anymore. He just stood there and looked at Jasmin helplessly, gulping down the sobs that kept rising in his chest.

"You're not a bad person, Alexander. I know that. But you're making things so hard for yourself. And then you go and do this. And I just don't know why."

He wanted to rush over to her, drop on his knees before her, implore her, and tell her that the affair was over and hadn't meant a thing. But he couldn't. He couldn't move and his lips wouldn't let the words pass.

Jasmin got up from the chair and pressed on: "Why do you do this to me? Why are you doing this to yourself?"

She looked at him, her gaze a plea for answers. Alex pressed his lips tight and looked away, blinking the tears away surreptitiously.

Jasmin's patience ran out. "I want you to leave now."

Alex looked up at her.

"Go!"

He still didn't move.

"Get out!"

Slowly, his head down, Alex finally walked out of the living room and into the hallway. As he pulled the door shut behind him, he could hear Jasmin sob loudly.

Halfway to his car he started walking faster and faster until he finally ran the last steps. He pulled open the door, jumped in, started the engine and drove off with screaming tires. Like a gangster in a car chase he went back and forth through the streets and alleys, trying to erase the memory of those moments in Jasmin's living room. Trying to undo things, unspeak words he'd spoken. But it was all there with him, in his head and in his heart, and it wouldn't let go. He felt it. For an instant he felt compelled to drive even faster, so fast that he might lose control of the vehicle. A way out. Instead, he decelerated. His vision was blurry because he had started crying. When he finally stopped, the sobs he had held back for so long broke loose violently.

Several minutes later he calmed down and wiped away the last of his tears. He was exhausted. His body felt like an immense weight, his head seemed empty, and the whole world around him like a dream. He watched himself turn the ignition key and drive off. At some point he found himself parked near the lake. He could see the ragged contour of the woods against the sky and the dull, black surface that would transform back into the lake with the first light of day. The night was too dark to make out anything else. Only some of the windows in the little subdivision around the lake. From somewhere between the houses he could hear the barks of a dog that had been left outside.

Alex settled back into the car seat, trying to get as comfortable as possible. He wanted to retreat into his fantasy of his house at the lake. He closed his eyes and tried to picture his house in the warm sunshine. He was eager to hear his kids play and laugh. He even allowed himself the dim hope that his wife would come up to him and take him in her warm embrace. But in vain. Instead of the house he saw wild flashes of images, too fast to recognize a lot. Jasmin, there and gone. Nicole. A dog came running toward him out of nowhere. But his peaceful dream oasis remained unreachable in this storm. Soon, all the images dissolved into the oblivion of sleep.

Early the next morning, Alex woke to the sounds of machinery. There was a crane on a plot of meadow by the subdivision, putting up billboards and signs. A few workers were directing the crane operator with hand signals.

Alex's eyes fell on the flowers that still lay on the passenger seat. A few of the blossoms had started to fade. He took the bunch and got out of the car. Having stretched a little, he walked down to the water. The surface was still absolutely glassy. The crisp air smelled of early morning. Alex looked once more at the flowers in his hand. Then he raised his arm behind his head and flung them away into the lake. The flowers made a splash as they hit the surface, bobbed up and down a few times, and started drifting apart in all directions. He sat on his heels and watched. A glance at his watch showed him that he'd be very late for work. He decided that he had just quit the job.

After a while Alex returned to his car. He wanted to go home and sleep a little more. As he drove off, he glanced in the rearview mirror at the crane and the construction workers and wondered what that was all about.

5

A cold wind was pushing the scattered clouds around the sky and the sun was too weak to warm up the afternoon. The congregation stood at the open grave, silent and with their heads bowed. Alex and his mother were in the first row. Stone-faced, they watched his father's coffin being lowered down.

The cemetery was large and spacious, separated from the rest of the world by a brick wall that ran all around. The funeral services were held in a chapel on a little hill. The graves were grouped into sections divided by well-kept gravel paths. The intersections of the larger paths were adorned with sculptures and fountains. In between and along the walls stood many trees. Their slight orange foliage announced the approach of fall. Alex had never been here before. For him, funerals and cemeteries in general had always been synonymous with deep sorrow and agony. Yet as he emerged from the chapel in the procession of mourners and took in the scenery, he felt a peculiar sense of peace. This place of eternal rest looked like a remote, silent garden sprouting crosses and headstones.

His mother stepped toward the open grave, dropped her bouquet of flowers on the coffin and murmured a prayer. Then it was Alex' turn. They both then remained on the side of the grave and saw the other mourners follow their example. To Alex' surprise, one of them was Jasmin. She joined the line of people giving their condolescences. As she came up to him, their eyes met briefly. It was the first time he'd seen her since leaving her house three weeks before. And once again, Alex saw the shimmer of tears in her eyes. This time, though, they shone with a warm light, not cold anger. Jasmin started to say something, but she was pushed forward by the people next in line and got lost in the crowd.

When the ceremony was over, many mourners remained standing in front of the chapel to offer words of sympathy to Alex and his mother. Finally, Alex stole away from the crowd. He went to his car, which he had parked outside the cemetery gates, and stood leaning against it. He had promised his mother to wait for her and drive her home.

"Your mom told me I'd find you here."

Jasmin was suddenly right beside him. He hadn't seen her coming because he was looking away from the chapel. Alex just looked at her. He was a little startled, that was one reason. The other was that he simply didn't know what to say.

She came very close and slung her arms around him.

"I am so, so sorry for your loss, Alexander."

He returned the embrace, drawing her close and feeling her body pressed to his. Jasmin sobbed quietly. They stood entwined until Alex felt Jasmin take her hands off his back. Only then did he release the embrace too.

"Thank you. I'm glad you came, Jasmin."

She wiped the tears from her eyes-

"Your mother called and told me about you father. My parents came to the funeral service, too. But they left right afterwards. They weren't sure whether you wanted to see them at the grave."

A smile stole over Alex' face and he shook his head.

"Tell them I'm very grateful they came. And I would have liked to see them there."

"I'll let them know."

Jasmin stood next to him, leaning against the car as he did. Their arms touched lightly. Alex watched his foot kicking at the pebbles on the ground.

"Your mother is a strong woman. She looks very composed and seems to be dealing admirably with all this. Truly amazing."

"I guess that's a way to put it."

"What do you mean?"

"I mean that both my parents have always been very good at 'managing' their emotions."

"I didn't get that impression when I talked to her on the phone. She seemed really struck by your father's death."

"Alex looked at Jasmin.

"Is that so? Maybe it was ill-timed because she was just in the middle of an important business deal?"

"Please don't say that, Alexander. She loved your father. She loves you, too. Very much. We had quite a long talk. She is sad to hear that we're having difficulties and she hopes that ..."

Alex interrupted her: "You talked to her about us?! That's none of her business. I told her we stopped seeing each other. That's all she needs to know."

"She is your mother, Alexander. She will always love and care about you. Whether you like it or not."

"Heavens, was there anything the two of you didn't talk about?"

"Don't just shut her out. She needs you. Now more than ever. She's lost someone she loved."

"I'm here, aren't I? All this production here – I'm doing that for her. Plus, it's not as if this death parted star-struck lovers."

"Every relationship has its ups and downs. You know that very well, Alexander."

"Oh, I'm not talking about ups and downs. Those two were a perfect match. They were very much alike. Almost frighteningly alike."

"So they were happy together."

"Happiness is such an ambiguoud term. My parents met in school. When they were teenagers in love they might have experienced something akin to love and passion. But that wasn't what their marriage was based on. The true connection between them was their shared life philosophy: grab what you can before someone beats you to it and enjoy life. And that's exactly what they did. Sometimes together, sometimes with other people. Their mutual understanding that what counts in life are professional success and a life of luxury and pleasure – that's what bound them together. They would probably not have married if they hadn't been expecting a child."

"For sure you're exaggerating. And I'm equally sure that they both loved you more than anything in the world and still do. Just like they loved one another. And now your father is gone forever."

"Pfff. Did you see her shed tears at the gravesite? In fact, was anyone there crying?"

"Alexander, who cares whether or not people are crying? That doesn't tell you anything about how they feel inside."

"You know, my father was what you'd call a pretty successful guy. Not a very good one, though. So why waste tears."

"Alexander! You mustn't say that. It was a nice funeral. Lots of people came."

"Some of them came because they're relatives. All the others are either his colleagues from the bank who most likely just wanted to make sure he's really gone, or my mother's employees who came to suck up to her."

Jasmin shook her head and blew her nose, discreetly drying her eyes while doing so.

"I can hardly recognize you, Alexander. How can you talk like that?"

"You know what he left me in his will? His hunting rifle. Can you imagine? The fucking rifle."

"He loved to go hunting. Maybe he wanted to leave you something that was dear to him."

Alex walked a few steps away from the car. Jasmin could hear him take three or four deep breaths. Then he turned around and stared at her intensely, his eyes narrow slits. Jasmin stood erect. Alex inhaled deeply and pointed toward the cemetery.

"With this gun he did the only decent thing of his entire life: He shot my dog with it!"

"He shot the family dog with his hunting rifle?!"

"It was MY dog."

Alex fought back tears but lost the battle. Once again he turned away and covered his eyes. Jasmin walked over to him and touched his shoulder. Instantly he took a step away. His shoulders twitched and though he made no sound, Jasmin could see he was sobbing. Patiently, she waited for him to calm down. Then she once again stood beside him and handed him a tissue. Alex took it and wiped his face with it.

"Come on, let's walk a little. Tell me about your dog."

They walked back towards the chapel and along the wall to the back of the graveyard. This way, they avoided meeting any of the mourners.

"His name was Buddy. He was a gift from my godfather for my fifth birthday. He was still a puppy when I got him."

"Was he the dog you took walking on the lakefront?"

"Yes. He wasn't very old then. Still liked to play and run around outside."

"And your father – he …"

"Shot him. In the end, it was the right thing to do. It's kind of a long story."

"Your mom is still busy with all those people. And I don't have to be anywhere."

Alex hesitated for a moment.

"Buddy was a good dog. When I got him, he was a sweet little pup, a bit clumsy. He chased anything I'd throw for him. Tennis balls, socks, Frisbees, empty plastic bottles – if it flew through the air, he'd try to catch it. Anything I threw too far, he usually wouldn't find. Nor would he ever bring anything back. Whatever he caught was his and got chewed up good and proper. It was also funny to play catch with him in the house. Maybe not funny-funny, but kind of amusing. Buddy always miscalculated his distance to stop so he would occasionally crash into the wall when he chased something. He didn't seem to mind that at all. All that mattered to him was that he got the ball. He really loved to play. And to be petted. When he tired of chasing balls, he would lie on the couch, his favorite spot, his head on my lap, and have me scratch his ears until he fell asleep. And he didn't just do that with me. He loved it when people came to visit. The more, the merrier – and the more hands to stroke and throw balls. He really enjoyed that. And he was very affable. Children, toddlers, grownups – he liked people in general and was never aggressive. Buddy was pure lust for life. He only started retrieving the objects I tossed him when he was fairly grown up. Well, he didn't really retrieve them. He would fetch the stick or whatever it was, but then he wouldn't let go of it. He'd either pull away when you tried to grab it or you'd have to chase him to get it. Once you'd get hold of the stick he wouldn't let go but fight you for it. So there we'd be, me with both hands on the stick, he holding on with his teeth. Though we both pulled and shook the other one pretty hard to get the stick, nobody ever got hurt. Even more than sticks, he loved tennis balls. Really was crazy for them. They'd fly in a high arch, bounce when they hit the ground, and they were just the right size for chewing. I think that dog heaven for Buddy is full of tennis balls.

It was back then, when he was in his dog teens, that we often went to the lake. Sometimes, my parents would come along on the weekends, but mostly it was just Buddy and me. We spent whole afternoons there after I came home from school. We'd go exploring or pretended we were all alone in the wilderness, fighting our way back home through the jungle. Those were great times. And of course we'd play fetch with his tennis balls. Buddy would run into the lake to fetch them without a moment's hesitation. I think that was the time I felt closest to him. Plus, he'd sleep in my room back then."

"That's exactly why I would have liked a dog. I would much rather have had a dog sleep in my room than my sister. That sounds so nice."

"Yeah, well, but those times passed. Somehow, everything changed. I couldn't say how it happened. Buddy was about one or two years old, an adult dog, and everything changed. I spent less time with him. I had to work harder for school, preferred playing football and video games to tossing balls. I'd rather watch TV than go out to the lake and I hung out with pals from school until my parents got home. Plus, Buddy wasn't the cuddly little puppy any more, but a big, imposing dog with more strength in his jaw than I had in my entire body. My parents also didn't like him on the couch anymore because his fur had grown long and he used to shed a lot. It took him quite a while to understand that he wasn't allowed up there anymore. My father finally used the paper to make him break the habit. He didn't hit him too hard, but it worked. Later, Buddy got his own dog house in the yard, which meant that he wasn't allowed to sleep in my room anymore. I think he spent weeks waiting at the door for us to let him in at night. The first couple of nights he would howl and bark out there, so my parents locked him up in the basement to keep him from waking the neighbors. After that he kept quiet when we left him outside at night. Finally, he got used to the dog house. The funny thing was that he'd bring all his toys, his tennis balls especially, into the little hut and then sleep in front of it. I must confess that we kind of neglected him back then. He'd basically become just another regular member of the family – someone who didn't deserve special care or attention. Someone just like one of us. Since nobody wanted to go for walks with Buddy anymore, my father started taking him along when he'd go hunting. That way he at least got out and around. Somehow, my father managed to teach him how to track and flush ducks and other animals. At least that's what he said. I don't believe that Buddy liked it. He'd usually hide in his dog house when they came back from their hunting trips. My father also tried to train him to be a watchdog. He wanted him to bark at strangers. But Buddy wouldn't do it, however my father tried to train and punish him – whether he'd starve him, call him names, or threaten to beat him. He was just a good dog. He only barked at the rolled-up newspaper or the stick in my father's hand. So my father gave up on the watchdog thing. Still, Buddy changed. I mean, if everything changes for you and nothing remains as it should be for you, it's only logical that you change, too. He spent most of the time alone in the garden back then. When I think back to that time, I see him lying in front of his dog house and chew on those tennis balls. That's basically all he did. I think he also used to sleep with a tennis ball between his paws. God, how he loved those balls. Maybe they helped him dream of the times when he used to chase them and fetch them from the lake."

Alex fell silent. They walked a while like that, in silence. Then he breathed in and out deeply. Jasmin took hold of his hands. He gave a start and looked at her. She nodded reassuringly. A weak little smile crossed his face.

"Then one day – I guess I was bored – I decided to play with Buddy. Toss him sticks or something. Like we did before. So I went out to the yard with a stick in my hand and over to his dog house. He lay there, chewing on a tennis ball. He looked up as he saw me coming. When I was only a few steps away, he leapt up. I didn't think it unusual. I thought he was happy to see me and was looking forward to playing fetch. So I walked over to him and stretched out my hand to stroke him. And then everything happened very fast: Buddy jumped forward and snapped at my hand."

"Oh! He did bite you?"

"No, he didn't bite. He only snapped. I was startled, of course, and pulled back my hand immediately. I think I also ran back into the house, crying. But that was only from shock. He didn't seriously hurt me. Buddy would never have seriously hurt me. He only snapped. You could see tooth marks on my hand, but there was no blood. They weren't even real scratches. It was only much later that it dawned on me why he'd done it. It was the stick. I had a stick in my hand."

"He was scared of the stick."

"Yes. He was scared. Or at least he didn't know what to do. He didn't bite me, he just snapped. He didn't mean any harm. I'm sure that he'd have loved to play with me, but he didn't know what I was up to. It had been so long since I had spent time with him and tossed a stick. So he associated that stick with a lot of things, but not with fun and games anymore. Back then, I didn't realize all that, of course. So when I told my parents about it, everyone was certain that Buddy has turned mean and we needed to do something about it. And what did we do?"

Jasmin stared at him, both shocked and questioningly.

"No, we didn't shoot him right away, if that is what you're thinking. My father may have thought about it, but we decided to try and 'resocialize'

Buddy. So we built an iron cage around his dog house and kept him in there. The cage was about the size of the ones they have in the dog pound."

Jasmin had stopped at a little wooden bench on an elevation in the back part of the graveyard. They sat down. From here they could oversee the entire cemetery with all the crosses and headstones, all the way to the chapel. Far off, two men were shoveling dirt in Alex' father's grave.

"That cage only made things worse. We also took away his toys – we figured if he didn't have them he'd be even gladder whenever one of us would come to play or just talk to him. But we only came out to him for the first few days. Afterwards, he'd only see us when we brought him his dog food. Buddy probably missed his tennis balls more than he did us. Plus, being locked up was synonymous with punishment for him. First the basement, now the cage. Even the best of intentions and a lot of care wouldn't have convinced him otherwise. To be honest … even now, all these years later, I'm not sure what we should have done. He wasn't the carefree, playful, vivacious dog he had once been. The way we had treated him had pushed him into a corner. He must have felt like an outcast in a strange world. And I have no idea how we could have brought him back. Maybe we should have just set him free. But who knows what would have become of him then. Anyway – he slept or lay there in his cage. We never regained his trust. On the contrary, he became increasingly unsettled whenever anyone came by to check on him or feed him. I think that Buddy knew that he had changed. He knew exactly that we wouldn't have been able to chase tennis balls anymore, however much he would have loved to. That must have made it even worse for him. He for sure felt he was about to lose his original essence. It was a struggle he couldn't win."

"With all due respect to Buddy and to you, don't you think you're overdramatizing a little?"

"Okay then, maybe he didn't notice or know any of that. He was just a dog, after all. But he was a bright one, and I'll always believe that he finally found a way out that didn't mean losing that struggle. Because one day, when my father stepped into his cage with a nice big chunk of meat for him, Buddy attacked him and bit him in the arm. Really tore into him. My father had to get stitches in the emergency room. As soon as he got home, he took his hunting rifle and shot Buddy. I didn't see him do it; they'd sent me up to my room. I didn't see Buddy's body, either. They got rid of it before I was allowed to get close to that cage. All that was left was that chunk of meat. Buddy hadn't touched it. As if he knew what was about to happen. As if he'd planned it. He wasn't mean. Buddy was a good dog. Things just went wrong. And I was partly to blame but ..."

"Alexander, you were just a child. What could you have done? Buddy liked you. Otherwise he would have bitten you."

"I should have spent more time with him. Toss him tennis balls, at home and on the lakeshore. I should have spared him the hunting trips and the basement. It's a typical case of being smarter afterwars. But there's no second chance, no way to make things better."

Jasmin put her arm around Alex. She kissed his cheek and rested her head on his shoulder. They sat like this and watched the men finish shoveling and leave. The place was completely still now, peaceful and silent.

"Do you miss him?"

"Very much. He was a great dog."

"I meant your father."

"Oh. Um. I don't know. I don't think so ... maybe not yet."

Jasmin got up from the bench. "Let's go back to the car."

Alex stood, she took his arm, and they walked off.

"Did you really tell your mother that we don't see each other anymore?"

"Yes. I also told here that I was the one who fucked up."

"That's not what I'm worried about. What I want to know is this: Do you really think it's over between us?"

"I cheated on you, Jasmin. I destroyed what was between us."

She stopped and bent to tie her shoes. When she straightened up again, her look was resolute.

"Are you still seeing that other woman?"

"No, of course not," Alex hastened to say. "That's been over for a long time."

Jasmin's expression didn't change. Her gaze was still fixed on him. "And do you want to stop seeing me, too?"

This surprised Alex.

"No! I want to keep seeing you, of course. But I cheated on you. And you told me to leave."

"Well, it doesn't take a genius to understand that I didn't want you around anymore that night."

"Right, but – did you want me around ever again, Jasmin? Would you have wanted me near you even if my father hadn't died?"

"Even then, Alexander. Did it really never occur to you to just ask me what I wanted? To get in touch again? To at least try to fight for me if I still meant something to you?"

"I wasn't sure … I was ashamed, and you cried … and I …"

Alex fell silent. Several times he tried to say something but the right words eluded him.

"Listen, Alexander. It's been a tough day for you and this is neither the time nor the place to discuss us. I, for my part, would like to give you another chance. But you have to earn it. You need to do something to deserve it. You hurt me pretty badly, so you have a lot of explaining to do. You have to set things right again."

Alex nodded. His lips formed a "thank you," but there was no sound. He tried to swallow the lump in his throat, but it was too big. Instead, he gave Jasmin a helpless look.
Finally she took his arm again and they walked on. Only after a couple of steps Alex was able to speak again.

"I could drive you home if you want. Maybe we could grab a bite somewhere."

"No, thank you, Alexander. My parents are waiting for me by the chapel. And you should spend the evening with you mother."

"It really would be no problem."

"You may take me out to dinner tomorrow."

"Good. I'll pick you up at seven."

Side by side they walked back to the chapel. The wind had died down; the sun had reached the horizon. The evening sky was a beautiful palette of pinks and reds.

They said goodbye where the path to the parking lot branched off.

"By the way, Jasmin, I've thought about the things we discussed with your parents on our last weekend together."

"Children?"

"Well, no. The other thing. God and all that."

"Oh. Okay. And?"

"Have you ever seen an ant farm?"

"Those boxes with glass sides that you fill with sand and dirt and ants?"

"Exactly. I built one back in school once. And I believe that if there is any higher being or whatever you want to call it, then we're his – or her – ant farm."

"You believe that we're tiny and unimportant?"

"Ants aren't unimportant just because they are so much smaller than us."

"You know what I mean."

"I'm not sure I do. Anyways, you build such an ant farm and then you put it somewhere. At first you're fascinated with the activity inside. You sit there and watch the ants do their things and you're really amazed by those little creatures. After some time, best case, you may give it an exposed spot, like a piece of decoration. But after a while you just grow used to them and forget about them. You turn to other, new things."

"Do you still have your ant farm?"

"No. At least I couldn't tell you where it is. I suppose my mother just threw it out at some point. All ant farms get thrown out sooner or later."

"Do you believe that we've been thrown out, then?"

"Who knows. That's no reason to despair, though. Just because ant farms get thrown out doesn't mean they can't start their very own huge and thriving colony at the dumpsite."

"You know, Alexander, a touch of respect of and a bit of humility towards life wouldn't hurt you at all. And you could also use a little more trust in humankind."

Alex seemed distracted by the people who were still standing in front of the chapel. He looked over to them and nodded absently. Then his gaze drifted up to the evening sky. Suddenly, as if he had caught hold of a thought up there that he wanted to hold onto, he stared at the ground. At last, he lifted his gaze again and met Jasmin's.

"I am sorry, Jasmin. I really regret what I've done to you. From the bottom of my heart."

"I know."

She placed a kiss on his cheek and turned to leave. Alex held her back.

"Are you sure you don't want me to drive you?"

"Absolutely. Just be there on time tomorrow."

6

It was much too early when Alex parked in front of Jasmin's building. He wanted to make sure he wouldn't be late. Besides, he needed a little time to find the right words to say to her. He had spent the previous day and half of the night thinking about all the things he wanted to tell her – and the right way to do it. So far, he hadn't come up with anything of much use. Actually, he had weeks to decide what to talk about with Jasmin. If he was really honest he had to admit that the reason he never called or tried to see her after his big confession wasn't that he thought she would not want him to. It was just easier for him this way. If she hadn't meant anything to him he could have just lied to her. He probably would never have told her about the affair in the first place. But now it would have been easier to just drop Jasmin. That would have spared him the whole horrible evening. On the other hand, he so much didn't want to let her go. Or rather, he didn't want her to let him go. Alex just didn't know how to deal with this new situation and with Jasmin. Being with her had been a challenge from the very start – one he didn't know how to handle. And yet, also the most wonderful gift. They'd met a little over a year ago, and Jasmin had confused and bewildered him from the very start.

It had been a summer evening more than a year ago. Back then, Alex had been working as a pizza delivery man. It had been a long day and the city was sweltering under a humid blanket of dusk. Alex was balancing a stack of hot pizza boxes on the crook of his arms and standing right in the middle of the sidewalk, sweating. People pushed and walked around him. Everyone seemed tired and in a hurry to get home. They smacked into him or cursed him whenever it was too crowded to move around him. Alex didn't care. He was beat. The hot humidity weighed on him like a ton of bricks. He fumbled to fish the bill with the delivery address from his jeans pocket, again, and stared up the dirty facade of the building. Wrong house, wrong street. Again. Alex shook his head and looked up at the windows in the building once again, as if deliberating if he should just take the pizza up there and hand it to whoever happened to be there. There was no way he'd be on time at the correct address, anyway. His boss would tear him a new one and the pizzas would be deducted from his meager wages. He might even lose his job. So at least there was an upside to the whole shitty situation.

"You look like you're lost."

"And you look beautiful." At least, that was what he should have said to Jasmin that day. He'd come up with it one night days later when he went over the scene again and again in his mind. It still haunted him that he hadn't said it. It would at least have given her the impression that he was a witty guy who was on her level.

But instead, he'd turned towards the voice and just stared dumbly at Jasmin, who had stopped in the milling crowds and smiled at him.

She was so beautiful. Standing there, calm and serene amidst the crowd, just smiling.

Try as he might, Alex couldn't remember what she was wearing that day, however often Jasmin told him that she'd just come from her job as a pediatrician in a nearby hospital and was still in her work uniform. All he remembered was that she was amazingly beautiful and had smiled at him.

"What is it you're looking for?" Jasmin had asked him.

Alex still could only stand and stare at her. He heard her voice, but her words didn't seem to get through to him.

"Which address are you looking for?" she asked once more, pointing to the piece of paper in his hand.

Finally, Alex unfroze. "How do you know I'm looking for an address?"

Jasmin's smile grew into a gentle chuckle. "Well, let's see: it says 'Pizza Flash' on your shirt, you're holding a stack of pizza boxes and you seem to be checking building numbers. So I deduced that you're looking for the right address to deliver your pizzas. Am I wrong?"

Alex blushed. "No, of course not. You're right. I'm delivering these. Or trying to."

Jasmin nodded, still smiling. That friendly, honest, oh-so-beautiful smile. She didn't make fun of him, she didn't patronize him, there was neither gloating nor irritation – just that beautiful smile. Pure. Unsullied. Beyond words. Gorgeous.

"May I?" she said, taking the note from him. From that moment on until the pizza was delivered, Jasmin didn't leave his side. She didn't know the address, either, so she just stopped one passerby after another until she found someone who gave her directions. Alex felt both impressed and slightly embarrassed.

Much later, Jasmin told him how much she had been impressed by him that day. Or rather, what an impression he'd made on her. Apparently, she had watched Alex from her office window before she stepped up to him. Several times he had moved out of her range of vision and then returned. After a while, she was intrigued and couldn't stop observing him. All those people milling about him, and Alex in the midst of it all. He'd just stood there, she said, looking up and around him, walking off and coming back, seemingly uncaring what the crowd of passersby thought of him and not even noticing them pushing and shoving and swearing at him. He'd been so sweet, she said. So out of place. And yet determined to finish what he came for. But also lost, almost helpless. All that had obviously made quite an impression on her. Alex never really knew how he felt about that. Mostly confused and bewildered.

Just like he felt now.

It was time. He should go and ring her bell. Alex' innards melted and his entire body seemed to deflate. Maybe, if he sat very still and didn't move a muscle, it would all just pass.
Coward.
Finally he pulled himself together and got out of the car. He needed to see her. That much was certain. He walked over to her door and rang the bell. When he heard the door being unlocked from the inside and saw the knob turn, he wished once

more that he'd just driven off while he still could. Out to the lake. He could be lying there now in his future garden and wait for the stars to come out.

"Hello, Alexander, good to see you." Jasmin gave him a kiss on the cheek.

Alex nodded, slightly embarrassed and absent-minded. He looked at her for a moment. She stood there and smiled at him. Beautiful.

"Shall we?" she said and put a hand on his arm. Together they walked over to Alex' car and drove off.

Jasmin was in a good mood and couldn't stop talking. She seemed set on telling him every little thing he might have missed over the past few weeks. At first, Alex was grateful and relieved. Jasmin's incessant babbling meant that he could remain quiet. And also that she obviously didn't see a necessity to discuss the state of their relationship. Maybe she thought it wise to move on and let bygones be bygones. He started to relax. He smelled her perfume. It had spread inside the car, a wonderful scent. Meanwhile, Jasmin told him the latest about her parents, her job at the hospital, and the little bookstore she had recently discovered and wanted him to see. Now and then,

Alex nodded and demonstrated his interest with the appropriate questions. Not that he had much interest. But he really felt comfortable and wanted Jasmin to keep talking. He enjoyed listening to her. Her voice was like gentle waves that lapped at his ears and rocked his mind into a sweet state of nothingness. Jasmin always had this gift of transporting him into another world. It was as if her physical presence was enough to alter his mind. It felt incredibly good to be near her again. Almost like their first night. The memory Alex treasured most wasn't of the first night they made love, but the first time he spent the night at Jasmin's. They dated a few times after their first meeting on the street. Alex couldn't really recall those dates. They must have been pretty casual, and contrary to his usual pattern, he hadn't ended up in bed with Jasmin. So that night they met for dinner, Alex picked up Jasmin at home. She wasn't ready yet, so she asked him in and he waited in the living room while she did whatever women do in her bathroom or bedroom. When she came back into the living room, Alex had fallen asleep on the couch. He could not recall every detail of that evening, but he knew that when Jasmin finally woke him, she had prepared dinner for them and set the table. After they finished eating she sat with him on the couch and let him rest his head on her lap. Then she started talking, telling him this and that, but he soon fell asleep again. Try as he might, he couldn't remember ever having felt so wonderful before. Or after, for that matter. It had to have been the maximum level of snugness a person could feel. Only when he was with Jasmin, as he was now, did he ever come close to it.

Now, however, the feeling was slowly, but surely giving way to a very sobering sense of shame, which caught up with him even today, giving him no room for escape. He would have preferred not to remember anything else about that night. But the truth was that he had finally come to blows with his boss at the pizza place that day and had subsequently been fired. After that, he didn't know what to do with himself until his date with Jasmin, so he called his father. He still did not know why he did that. He usually just let his parents call him. And from that day on, he strictly upheld that rule. But back then, his father had been in the hospital after his first heart attack, and Alex had not yet been to visit him. As luck would have it, his mother was there in the hospital when Alex called. So the phone call turned into the usual discussion: how could he live like that, what were his plans for the future, and so on. Alex would have loved to just hang up or find some excuse to end the call. Instead, he tried to explain and justify his life before he gave up and let the whole sermon just wash over him. He was not even sure whether he ever found out how his father's health was. He never did get to visit him in the hospital. By the time he arrived at Jasmin's place that night, he was tired and emotionally drained. He probably should have called off their date. But the prospect of seeing her had been a comfort. Actually, he wanted to tell her everything and ask for a rain check. But then, she had been so great, the whole evening had been so wonderful, so he just stayed. And it had been amazing. Up to the moment when he woke the next morning, still lying on her couch. His head wasn't in her lap anymore; instead, she had placed a pillow under his head and covered him with a blanket before she went to bed. Alex remembered the warm wave of feeling absolutely safe and carefree that rose inside him as he awoke. As soon as his mind started to process the previous day, though, hot lashes of shame whipped him into full alertness. Pummeled by guilt, he fled Jasmin's apartment. He had used Jasmin the night before, allowed her to soothe his ego and make him forget all the mess of his life instead of taking her out for a nice dinner as promised. And that wasn't all. He also failed to mention all that happened. He hadn't told her that he was nothing but an unemployed loser with no future. She should have kicked him out; that would have been best. Instead, Jasmin had been wonderful and he had enjoyed it. And that was why he had to creep out of her apartment at the crack of dawn. At that moment and in the hours that followed, Alex wouldn't have dreamt that Jasmin might ever want to see him again, much less allow him back into her life.

Yet, after some time had passed and his early-morning panic had subsided, he changed his mind. The previous night had been too great, even without any lovemaking. So, he called her a few hours later and told her he had to be at work very early and didn't want to wake her. After all, she had done so much the night before. He thanked her profusely, apologized for his behavior, and asked for a chance to make it up to her and finally take her out for that promised dinner. Ever since that phone call, Alex had been unsure whether Jasmin was an angel or maybe he himself the devil. One thing was clear, though: she had always been much too good for someone like him.

They met again that same day and became an item. He didn't tell her about losing his job until much later, or rather, he told her that he started working at the sandwich store. And shortly afterwards he started seeing Nicole.

"I was scared!" he suddenly erupted. Jasmin jumped and looked at him.

"I was scared, okay?" he repeated, turning jerkily on to a smaller road and stopping the car.

"I was petrified, Jasmin.""

"Huh?" Not only did she not understand what Alex was talking about, she was also still shaken up by his sudden outburst and hazardous maneuver.

"I was scared. That's why I started the affair."

"Okay. I was going to wait until after dinner, but if you are ready to talk about it now, so be it."

"I never wanted to hurt you. Never. It was just … it all happened so suddenly. This thing with us was just too … too good. That's what got me scared."

"What we had was too good so you had sex with another woman?"

"Yes. No. Yes. In a way. It just got me scared."

"What exactly was it that scared you?"

"You know, I'd also like to be convinced that there is more in life than reason would allow me to believe. I want to be fully certain that love is more than just brain chemistry. I want to know for sure that there is a deeper meaning to life, and that we can do great things here on earth."

"So?"

"I don't know how."

"And you figured an affair would help?"

"No. No, of course not."

Alex looked out the side window as if for something to help him clear his mind and explain what he was trying to say. Jasmin waited patiently for him to turn back to her.

"Maybe it was fear of failure, of disappointing you."

"Well, that fear seems to have been justified. You did disappoint me. Very much so."

"I know. But that's not what I meant."

"Then what is it you meant?"

"You are so unlike anyone I ever met before. Your family is unlike any I ever knew. Everything about you and around you is different."

"Well, that goes for every human being, I guess. We are all different."

"Yes, sure. But…"

"But what?"

Again, Alex paused and turned his head, now staring at the steering wheel in front of him. He drummed on it with his fingers. Several times he seemed about to say something but instead shook his head, caught in an inner struggle. Finally he drew a deep breath.

"Your way of being in love. The way you look at me. The way you look at … life. It scared me."

"I still don't understand."

"You are such a wonderful person. Whenever I'm with you, I feel like I'm a good person, too. You make me feel like someone who is good."

His eyes welled up. Jasmin noticed and gave him a moment.

"And what's the problem with that?"

"The problem with that? Jasmin, I'm not a good person! I'm not like you. Not even close. I don't know how to handle it. You're the best thing that ever happened to me, but I don't know how to deal with that."

"There are probably better ways of dealing with it than starting an affair. You could have talked to me. Like you do now. Silly boy."

Alex stared ahead into empty space. "I know. I am sorry. I would have loved to be good enough for you, but I'm not."

Jasmin gaped at him. She gasped for air and seemed about to start screaming, but her mind was in tumult, so she could not say anything for a few seconds. She waited until her thoughts stopped racing.

"Do you really think I would want to be with you if I didn't think as highly of you – or even more so – than you of me? You are a good person! You may be very good at hiding it sometimes, but deep inside you're the best person I've ever met. You silly, silly man! How can you even think such a thing? How can you feel that way? What did you let them beat into you? Look at me!"

"Jasmin, I really did not want to hurt you. Honestly. I just panicked. It was a stupid, a horrendously stupid mistake. I regret it so deeply you can't imagine. I want to apologize for hurting you, and I truly hope that you'll find it in you to forgive me."

Jasmin's eyes searched his face. A million feelings raced through her: compassion, anger, astonishment, perplexity, affection – to name only a few. His eyes still looked scared. She met his gaze, but he did not falter. So lost and still so determined. Finally, she felt gentleness overcome her anger and a slow tide of love rise within her.

"I will not tolerate such a thing ever again. And I never again want to hear you say that you are not a good person or not good enough for me. Is that clear?"

"Absolutely."

"If there is something you do not like or feel uncomfortable with, you will just have to talk to me."

"I will. I will be better. I promise."

"What about now? Are you scared now?"

"I'm still petrified. But what scares me even more is the thought of losing you."

"Let's work on it then. Show me that you are serious and that I am your future."

"I will do anything to make it so. I promise."

"I mean right now. Show me now."

"What do you mean? Here, in the car?"

Jasmin could not suppress a giggle.

"Well, well, seems like you're not a good person after all – what dirty deed did you have in mind? Don't look at me like that! I'm just teasing you. What I meant is that you should get your job at the bank back and finish your training."

Now Alex was really confused. What did his training have to do with it? Yet he certainly did not want to start a discussion about that.

"I'll call them Monday and ask if they'll take me back."

"See, you *are* a good person. And now kiss me, stupid."

That evening they did make it to the restaurant. Their dinner wasn't a making-up celebration, as

Jasmin stressed. What they celebrated, she said, was the beginning of their future together, which they toasted with champagne.

Alex did not like champagne, but he did not want to jeopardize the beginning of their future. After the first glass, he switched to red wine. He didn't dare to go for beer, his usual favorite. That evening he nevertheless had quite a lot of wine because he also didn't forget to celebrate his new, old job.

When they had finished their starters, Jasmin continued telling him about her job and her life in general, continuing where she'd left off when Alex had interrupted her in the car. She talked and he listened, just like old times. Her voice and the wine soon rekindled that warm feeling of wellbeing in Alex and dulled his senses. A pleasant heaviness settled upon him like a slow release. He looked at Jasmin. Her eyes were beautiful. Her lips so soft. Soft and supple. He knew exactly how their touch felt. He saw her lips move, but her voice and the words that came over those lips faded into the background. They became mere ambient noise. The restaurant lights became specters. Alex was standing at the lakeshore in front of his house. Someone was waving to him from the garden. He stepped closer. Now he could see it was a woman. She was waving and calling something. Now he heard that she was calling his name. He wanted to enter the garden, but when he bumped into the gate of the fence surrounding the garden, he was back at the table in the restaurant, looking into Jasmin's questioning eyes. "Alexander, the waiter just asked if we want anything else?"

Only now Alex noticed the waiter standing beside the table and looking at him expectantly.

"What do you think? Are you up for dessert?" Jasmin asked.

"Yes, why not. Sweets for my sweet."

After dessert they took a cab to Jasmin's place. Alex went to get his car the following day and stopped at his apartment on the way back to Jasmin to pick up some clothes and his toothbrush. She had asked him to spend a few nights at her place.

When he went to the bank, they gave him back his job without asking questions. Alex supposed that had to do with his father's recent death. But that worried him less than he'd anticipated. What he cared most about was Jasmin. He did not want to disappoint her again. No, he wanted to show her how serious he was. He hated having to wear a suit to work instead of jeans and t-shirts. But every morning when he left for work he could see how proud and happy she was. Surely he would get used to the suits and all the rest. After all, other people did too. And if it was so important to Jasmin, it could not be wrong or too difficult. The job itself wasn't all that bad. At the beginning he had to do menial work for others, of course, but they soon told him that he had quite a future ahead of him at the bank if he kept at it -- just like his father had. So Jasmin was happy, he made good money, and his career prospects seemed to be good. All as it should be. Plus, Jasmin assured him that she would be there for him if things ever got too hard for him. She said that it might not always be smooth sailing, there could be difficult times ahead where he might feel in a rut. But she would still be there for him and help him get through such crises. Though he could not quite imagine it yet, he felt that he might finally be on the right path to his house at the lake.

Alex' new life as a white-collar worker needed some getting used to, but they were good times nevertheless. It was as if he and Jasmin had fallen in love all over again. They could not get home fast enough after work, the nights were much too short, and they often talked on the phone during the day. Well, it was mostly Jasmin who did the talking. Alex mainly listened and immersed himself in her apparently limitless enthusiasm for every little thing life had to offer. Sometimes she asked him about his office mates or other harmless stuff, like what he had for lunch – questions he duly answered. Otherwise their life together consisted of lovemaking, kissing, and discovering their world together all over again. Every walk around the neighborhood was an exploration of things and impressions hitherto unseen. Every little day trip was a journey of experiences that hit Alex to the core like epiphanies. Every moment together was a moment out of time.

Alex even started to enjoy the shopping trips Jasmin asked him to take – and she didn't have to ask long these days. He began to see why extended shopping wasn't just a tedious waste of time. One did not have to march into the next-best store, grab a pair of pants in the right size, pay without trying them on, and leave as fast as possible. Jasmin showed him how much fun it was to sit back and watch her model little black dresses, elegant evening gowns, and fancy high heels, even though they had no intention of buying anything. Once, they were even about to get kicked out of a lingerie store for indecent behavior. When the roles were reversed and he was the one doing the modeling, however, it was a little harder to enjoy. Trying on smoking jackets and too-tight leather pants for Jasmin's enjoyment took a big portion of stoicism.

And today was one of those days – Jasmin was determined to buy Alex some new shirts. He usually got his shirts in the same store. Always. He knew his size, he knew where to find the shirts, he could just have popped out to get them. But Jasmin had heard of this one particular label and this new store, and maybe, she said, they had some cool new patterns and colors there. Alex did not mind that it had taken hours. The main thing was that now he walked through the emptying streets with the shopping bags in one hand and a tired, but happy Jasmin on his other arm. They were just debating what to have for dinner when Jasmin grabbed Alex's arm and pulled him over to the other side of the street. She stopped in front of a jeweler's shopping window where he could see a display of rings. Jasmin smiled at him.

"This isn't the first time you have come by her, is it, sunshine?"

"Well … almost the first time."

"So – which one do you like best?"

Jasmin pointed at a subtly elegant, white-gold ring shaped like a flower. In the heart of the blossom there glowed a not-too-small, round, pure, white, brilliant cut diamond.

"That one is beautiful, no doubt about that."

"Isn't it?"

"And very, very pricey. Might take a while before I can afford it." Alex tried to pull Jasmin gently away from the window.

"But at least it gives you a good reason to go to the office every morning."

He stopped and stared at her, surprised and a little disbelieving. His reaction made Jasmin chuckle.

"Don't you worry, it does not have to be today or tomorrow."

She caressed his cheek, pulled his head down, and kissed him. Then she gently bit his earlobe and whispered: "But you could move in with me, though."

Two weeks later, the moving van was parked in front of Alex's building. When they were looking at the jeweler's window, Alex had been amused by Jasmin's subtlety in planning the whole thing – if it indeed had been a plan. Now, on his moving day, he was fascinated and elated that it was actually happening, and happening fast. Jasmin had hired the movers, bought boxes, arranged for the disconnection of his utilities and phone line, and sent address change notes to his friends and family. She'd also given Alex lots to look forward to: she had pampered him with the whole program, from dusk till dawn, as it were. And she had told him again and again how happy she was – how happy he made her. The whole procedure left Alex feeling almost as if he wasn't moving, but being moved. Be that as it may, they were only making things official – after all, he had basically already moved in with Jasmin, so this was just the logical next step.

Nevertheless, Alex felt strange standing in his empty apartment and taking a last look around. Well, almost empty. There was still one box propping open the main door. It was windy outside and with the windows and doors open, there was a draft. It was a small place, just one bedroom, a kitchen, and a bathroom. But it had been his small place. His home for the past few years.

His kitchen and bathroom had been 'typical bachelor style,' as Jasmin had always said when she came over. The furnishings were spartan and not even close to covering the bare necessities as a woman would define them: cabinets, rugs, baskets, shower curtains, too many dishes, cutlery, appliances, etc.. All that stuff that Alex found superfluous. His combined living room/bedroom had been just as sparsely furnished: a bed, a silent butler for his suits and shirts, a few boxes for the rest of his cloths, a couch, a little shelf for his TV and stereo and a table with three chairs. That was all he needed to feel at home. Unlike Jasmin, who had always told him what was missing at his place, namely plants, pictures, bookshelves, souvenirs, and all kinds of "decorations", or whatever they were called. That was why they hardly ever met here. It was also the reason why the move went so quickly. Sure, it also helped that they had thrown out the few pieces of furniture he owned. After all, Jasmin's apartment was "fully furnished", so it made no sense to keep the stuff. In the end, all Alex had to pack was his clothes. It took him no more than half an hour.

Alex picked up the last of the boxes. It was full of t-shirts. Placed on top was his father's hunting rifle. He kept it under his bed. He wanted to throw it out with the bed and all the rest, but Jasmin wouldn't allowed it. Through the open window he could hear her calling him from down on the street. He ignored her. Yes, he liked the idea of moving in with Jasmin and starting a new life with her. But leaving here was harder than he'd expected. Again, she was calling for him. From the stairs this time. He cast a last glance around the room and made sure he left nothing behind. Jasmin was standing in the door to his apartment now. Their eyes met. She smiled and gave him a sympathetic nod. Then she took the box from him and disappeared down the stairs. Finally, Alex drew a deep breath, took one last, good look around, and searched his pockets for the keys to the apartment. He was supposed to drop them in the landlord's mailbox. The moment he stepped into the stairwell, still looking for the keys, there was a sudden gust of wind and the apartment door slammed shut with a loud bang. Startled, Alex jumped, his whole body suddenly alert. He wheeled around, grabbed the doorknob and shook it several times. The door had clicked shut and wouldn't open. For a moment, Alex stood motionless in front of the shut door, lost in thought.

Then he remembered that Jasmin had the key because she had locked up for the movers that morning.

For the first days after the move, Alex felt like a piece of furniture that eventually somehow did make it over here from his old place: he didn't fit in with the rest of the furniture, there wasn't really enough space for him, and he would most likely be discarded pretty soon. What made things extra hard was that he couldn't for the life of him understand why he should feel so out of place now – after all, he had for all intents and purposes been living here at her place long before the official move. It wasn't Jasmin, either. On the contrary – for her, his moving in seemed to be a liberation, and her affection growing stronger. Fortunately, she did not even seem to notice that Alex occasionally avoided her. Sometimes he stayed in the office late, though he had started to mind spending so much time at this kind of job. But in the evenings, the office was usually empty, which made it easier. Now and then, he went to a bar to watch a game. He did it just to avoid spending the whole night in the apartment with Jasmin. Plus, drinking a couple of beers helped him deal with the whole situation until he would get used to it someday.

So when the neighbors stopped by to ask whether he and Jasmin could look after their dog for the weekend, he was more than willing. The neighbors had to go to some family shindig, a wedding or something. Alex hadn't paid attention, but the fact was that they couldn't take their dog, and that was good for him. He hoped the dog would be a distraction. And that it would relax things in Jasmin's apartment, which now was his apartment, too – though he felt the walls closing in on him, even if Jasmin didn't seem to see it.

When the neighbors finally dropped the dog off in the early evening that Friday, Alex could not have been more disappointed. The mutt just walked into the apartment and dropped down in a corner of the room. The neighbors assured Alex that he was very friendly and low-maintenance. As long as he had food and water, Alex and Jasmin would hardly notice that he was there. Plus, he was very well trained and would follow their commands.

The dog really did not seem to mind spending the weekend at a strange place. He did not seem to mind anything at all. He just lay there motionless and stared into space. Alex sat on the couch and watched the dog. He had expected a playful, vivacious animal. Or at least an excited one. One who needed attention and promised distraction. A bouncy fellow who wanted to run around. An exuberant, almost unrestrainable bundle of energy. With sparkling eyes, alert ears, a proud posture, and lust for life. Not just another piece of furniture – one that smelled of old dog. No wonder his owners didn't want to take him anywhere.

"I'm taking him for a walk. Want to come?"

Jasmin put the dog on the leash.

Alex considered for a moment, then he said: "Yes. Let's drive out to the lake."

"To the lake? Don't you think we can take him for a walk right here?"

"Sure. But maybe he'll wake up and get a move on if we take him to the lake. Let's see if he's any good at duck hunting."

"What if he doesn't like to be in the car?"

But Alex had already grabbed the car keys and stormed out.

During the entire drive, the dog lay calm and impassively on the back seat.

He only raised his head for a second when they arrived at the lake and Alex braked abruptly only to turn the car and drive straight back home. Alex ignored Jasmin's confused, questioning gaze and murmured something about an urgent phone call he had forgotten. She didn't ask any questions as Alex drove home much too fast, his face clouded and stony. She did not want to irritate him any further.

Down at the lakeshore, large earthmovers had started digging up Alex's land. Metal rods on the ground marked the outline of gigantic construction.

7

"Hello, Bob. It's me, Alex."

"Alex? Alex who?"

"We went to high school together. Last row, table by the window."

"Oh, Al! Hey, Al, how are you? All fresh?"

"Pretty good, thanks. How about you?"

"Can't complain. Business is good. Just had a new swimming pool built in the backyard. With a jacuzzi! You should come by sometime and check it out. We'll have some cold beers and a steak fresh from the barbecue and talk about old times."

"Sure. What I'm calling you about is …"

"Hey man, it's really been a while since I last saw you! Back then you'd just dropped out of college and started some job at that mail order place, packer or something. Are you still doing that?"

"Haven't for a while now."

"The broads there must have been hot and ready, huh? I mean, the work must be so fucking boring, you gotta get your thrills somewhere, right? Knowing you, you made the best of it."

"No, actually I didn't."

"You know what also gets the chicks all hot and ready? A Jacuzzi. Man, ever since word got round that I've installed one of those babies, I have to fight the chicks off with a stick. There have already been some memorable water games, if you know what I mean."

"I can imagine."

"You really should come by. I'll introduce you to some babes and off you go into the jacuzzi. Party a little, you know what I mean? I got everything you need to quench your thirst and powder your nose. No questions asked."

"Thanks Bob. I'm actually calling about ..."

"Fuck, man, you're not married or anything, are you?"

"No, I'm not married."

"Glad to hear it. Why marry, huh? If God had wanted us to marry, he wouldn't have created such an abundance of beautiful girls. That's what I think."

"If you say so."

"Sure, man! You know what's best about being a man? We can knock up a little twenty-year-old even when we're ninety. Who says heaven isn't a place on earth, huh?"

"Maybe, Bob. I wanted to talk to you about the property, though."

"Property? What property?"

"Your property down by the lake. The one I wanted to buy from you. A piece of it."

"Oh, that. What about it?"

"I was down at the lake recently. Saw that there were earthmovers."

"Oh, that was fast."

"What was fast?"

"They were fast starting construction. We sold the land to that rich foreign guy. Heaven knows where he's from. One of those countries with the unpronounceable names. Anyway, doesn't matter because he paid double the price for the property. Was dead set on buying it and building some concrete bunker for tourists. "

"Did you sell him the entire plot?"

"Sure, man. Double the price! How else do you think I paid for my pool? Not to mention the cars and the girls."

"Bob, I wanted a piece of that land. You knew that. We talked about it."

"Oh, yeah, right. You mentioned something along those lines."

"And yet you sold all of it?"

"Come on, Al. You were never serious about that, were you? What did you want to do with the land?"

"Well, whatever one does with a piece of land. Build a house, make a garden, sunbathe, and enjoy the view."

"Yeah, sure. You know, I don't see you as the kind of guy who settles down for good. And you had years to make me an offer."

"Somehow, I never got around to it."

"Well, now it's gone. Whatever. Be honest, Al, do you really believe you would eventually have bought it?"

8

On the ride home from the lake, neither of them
spoke a word. Alex parked the car in their street,
jumped out and hurried into their apartment.
Jasmin took the dog for a walk around the block to
give Alex some time to calm down. He was clearly
upset by something, though she didn't know what
it was. Still, she was curious to find out what had
made him so mad. She would have liked to ask
him in the car, but his mood had scared her a little.
So she figured it was best to give him some time
and wait until he was ready to explain what was
wrong. Jasmin knew that he had a lot to deal with
these past weeks – his new job, the move, his
father's death. Yet he also felt disappointed by the
way he behaved. That he'd shut her out.

When she came home, the door was open and the
apartment dark and silent. She shook her head
resignedly and took the leash off the dog, which
went straight into his corner and disappeared into
the dark. Jasmin was sure that Alex had left to deal
with whatever it was by himself. When she
switched on the light in the living room and saw
Alex sitting at the table, she jumped. He was
sitting with his elbows propped on the open
telephone book, his face in his palms. Scattered on

the floor next to his chair were the remains of the telephone.

Slowly, Jasmin sat down at the table and asked him what happened. Alex raised his head. His eyes were bloodshot. Without needing further encouragement, he told her about the plot of land by the lake where a hotel was now being built. He told her that he'd planned to build a house at the exact same spot. On this plot that had once belonged to his schoolmate and that he had always wanted to buy because he wanted to build a house there. Only now, someone else had bought the land. And then he went farther back and talked about his afternoons at the lake with Buddy. He told her about all the times he'd been there, how he loved the lake, and that he'd always wanted to build a house there. But now the land was sold and they were building a hotel instead.

At last, he fell silent. Tears filled his eyes. Helpless he looked into Jasmin's eyes, his gaze a question. And just before the tears could run down, Jasmin leant over the table and took hold of Alex's hands.

"There are other places. We can build a house somewhere else."

"If I'd met you before, I might really have bought that plot."

"Alexander, listen to me. There are other plots of land."

"Is it bad that I didn't buy it in time, Jasmin?"

"No, of course not. Don't talk nonsense. It's just a piece of land."

"It was my piece of land by the lake."

"I believe that if you had really wanted it that much, and could seriously have imagined building a house and living there, you would have bought it long ago. Maybe things turned out the way they were supposed to."

For a moment, Alex stared at Jasmin, stone-faced. Like a rock climber hanging over a deadly abyss, he tried to find a strong foothold in Jasmin's eyes, something to hold on to and pull himself back up. When he found nothing, his tension loosened. The tears ebbed from his eyes, his gaze grew empty and tired. At last he smiled gently and squeezed Jasmin's hands.

"Let's have a bite to eat and snuggle up in front of the TV before we go to bed, Jasmin. I'm dog-tired."

It was true, Alex was exhausted. Still, he slept little that night. When they went to bed, he turned his back on Jasmin, who had her arms around him, and pretended to fall asleep. But he lay awake the whole night, desperate for the escape of sleep. He tried not to think about his conversation with Bob and the land that had been sold. His land by the lake.

But every time he managed to fend off the flow of thoughts behind a wall of oblivion or repression, Bob's voice and the images of the earthmovers down at the lake would spill over like little waves. Their constant onslaught would wear down his entire defense wall, flooding his mind and keeping him awake. When he finally did manage to escape into an uneasy slumber, it was Jasmin and her insistence that there were "other pieces of land" that jolted him back to full consciousness. In retrospect, and in the semi-dream state of his exhaustion, her attempt at comforting him seemed more like a road sign into a threatening, unknown wasteland. For the first time since he'd met her, he had a chilling of uneasiness around her.

For the remainder of the weekend, Jasmin and Alex tried to get their neighbor's dog to play inside a little and not jump away scared when they rolled a tennis ball toward him as enticement. They also tried to get him to be a little more interested in his surroundings when they went on a walk, encouraging him to sniff trees and fire hydrants. To no avail. All he did was dump his business and head back home. But at least their attempts gave them something other to talk about than the lake and the land.

Though Alex's thoughts kept going back to his phone call with Bob and the property, he didn't bring it up again. One reason was that he didn't feel there was much left to talk about. The other was that Jasmin was probably right – it wasn't the only piece of land in the world. They would find something, somewhere. When they were ready. Besides, his life was otherwise great. He was with Jasmin, they lived together in a nice apartment, he had a good job, and at some point in the not-too-distant future he would drop on one knee, pop the question and put a very expensive ring on her finger. Basically, everything was much better than he would ever have imagined. It was the way he had always tried to imagine. Everything seemed to fit into that perfect, wonderful picture.

Except for him. That he could not deny.

The person he'd imagined in his own perfect idea of his life had always been someone else. Not the real him. The imagined him. It was the idea of himself. The better Alex. And this set him free of his desires, free to be part of his perfect ideas. His imaginary, ideal self always fitted in perfectly with the ideal world. The one doing the imagining, the real Alex, was left feeling the misfit – and he comforted himself with the dreams of his ideal self. The excitement and upheaval of the past days and weeks drowned the real Alex's feeling of being not quite right. Now, though, having settled into new or old routines and habits, the feeling rose to the surface again and he could not shake it off. That wonderful awesomeness Jasmin had brought into his life from the very first second had always instilled in him the feeling that he wasn't the right recipient for that great gift and didn't know how to deal with it. After their reunion, he had believed, or at least strongly hoped, that this feeling would eventually fade.

Instead, it had grown stronger. Ever since the incident at the lake, he'd become more and more conscious of it. It really scared him. But what scared him more was the thought that he might freak out and do something stupid again. He had already hurt and disappointed Jasmin terribly. He could not allow that to happen again. He must find a way to deal with his feelings. Jasmin meant everything to him. She was everything he ever wanted from life.

And yet he often stayed late at work. His bar visits became more frequent, too. And though he felt increasingly exhausted and hollow, he wasn't able to sleep soundly. Like this morning: he had laid awake for what seemed hours and then turned off the alarm clock before the set time. Afterwards he laid motionless and wide awake until it was well past time for him and Jasmin to get up. Only then did he turn on the radio. Now they would have to hurry off to work without time for breakfast.

Jasmin was irritated that they had overslept but all the more grateful to Alex for letting her use the bathroom first. He felt miserable about it. Not because he had tricked Jasmin into this rush, but because he felt he had no choice. No sooner had she disappeared into the bathroom than he hurried out of bed and into his clothes. He called his goodbye to her through the closed door, telling her he'd grab a coffee and a muffin on the way to the office. As he left the room, he heard her voice but didn't understand what she was saying.

Sitting behind the wheel of his car, he would have preferred to go anywhere else but work. Like every morning though, he dutifully headed towards the office. He had promised her, after all. And like every morning there was a traffic jam. Rows and rows of cars, like big steel lemmings waiting to get ahead. Smaller side streets branched off to the left and right, leading to clear roads after only a few blocks. Still, they all stood here, waiting for things to move along. A horn was blaring somewhere. There was always a horn blaring somewhere. And it never helped. This intersection was always jammed up at this time of day. Every morning. Everybody knew it. Everyone hated it. Every single day. Some hated it a little more, some a little less. And yet they would all be here again tomorrow. Same time, same place. New traffic jam. Someone would blow his horn. And it wouldn't change a thing. Why did Bob sell the damn land? It had been Alex's land. He would have bought it. Eventually he would have bought it. He grabbed the wheel so tight his knuckles were white. The car in front of him inched forward. Alex slammed one hand on his horn and screamed: "Move! Move and let me get out of here!" It didn't help.

Half an hour later, he drove up in front of the coffee shop. His anger and frustration had passed; he stood in line and waited. His outburst in the car had jolted him awake briefly, but now exhaustion descended on him with a vengeance. Tired, he shifted his weight from foot to foot. Standing in line seemed strenuous. Things at the coffee counter moved slowly, so Alex had plenty of time to deliberate what to get. He couldn't decide, listened to the orders of the other customers, and read the menu over and over again. What he really wanted was to go back to bed and sleep – not drink coffee to stay awake. What was the use of it, anyway? He would only drive to the office and do the same tedious tasks that didn't interest him in the least. All day long. Another customer placed his order and the line moved two or three steps forward.

We're shuffling in step like a chain gang, Alex thought. On closer looks, his chain gang mates also looked like they needed sleep far more than they did coffee. Instead, they would all guzzle down the caffeine so that they could function the rest of the day at their jobs. And at night, they would all come home, worn out and tired, only to get up again the next morning after too little sleep and stand here in line again with all the other pathetic jerks. Bullshit. Maybe that's why nobody here said a word until it was their turn to order. Nobody smiled, either. They all looked sleepy and beat. It wasn't Alex's first time in this particular place. He would often get a coffee on his way to the office because the brew they had at work was disgusting. Today though, the line seemed extraordinarily long and depressing. He was close to pushing the guy in front of him out of his way and just marching up to the counter. But he didn't. Instead he left without buying anything, walked back to his car, and drove to the office. He had promised her, after all. He would pull himself together and get through this day like so many others before. She meant everything to him. Or at least she was all that was left to him.

The morning in the office went unexpectedly smooth. Alex was so tired that he could just switch his mind to standby and do his job more or less automatically. The hours passed without anything affecting him at all.

It wasn't until he returned to the office building after getting a sandwich and walking around the block that he felt truly awake for the first time that day. It felt good. The events of the morning had faded into the distance and his memories of them seemed to have dissolved along with his exhaustion. Sometimes it felt as if he was spending his days in two different worlds. Alex smiled to himself. Maybe he and Jasmin would eventually end up in a world the both could inhabit. He liked thinking about it. The idea of settling a new world with her – preferably one they had all to themselves. He grinned wider. God, how she would hate him to take her there. A place with no other people in it was not exactly paradise to her. Well, at least their world should be one without traffic jams and coffee addicts in the morning.

Back at his desk, Alex wished he could just switch back into the robotic state of the morning, stare into space, and let the rest of the work day pass by. But now, he was too alert to slink back into near-unconscious work mode. Alex tried to stop his thoughts and return his focus to the task at hand. He just needed to function. He organized some paperwork. Tried not to think. It couldn't be all that bad. He could get used to it. Others did, didn't they? He had made a promise to Jasmin. But did "real" jobs really have to be like this? Was this what "real" life was like? Just disconnect and bear it. It made being human just a soulless imprisonment, minute after meaningless minute marching by, mercilessly in a long, straight, endless row, time wasted without salvation. Every man an island. Everyone his own microcosmos lost in the infinity of space. Or not even that, but just a slave of his microcosmos, condemned to exist as a fixed star orbited by the planets of pipe dreams that obstructed the view into the empty darkness beyond. This allowed us to be insensitive to our own powerlessness and blind to the disoriented activity going on in nothingness. We were wittingly or unwittingly held down by the ball and chain of civilization and what we took to be a natural, eternal order.

Again, Alex tried to shake himself out of the funk. He mustn't get lost in this maelstrom of thought. Spreading out the recently organized paperwork on his desk, he started sorting it through once again. Everything was already processed and just needed to be filed. But there wasn't anything else to do right now. He wished he'd been less productive in the morning. He stacked all the papers again and went over to the filing cabinet to stow them away, one by one. Looking over the cabinet, he could watch his colleagues. He tried to ignore them. Drifting microcosmoses. Shuffling about, talking in whispers. Dead faces.

It was the same wherever you went. It was just the true essence of being human.

Alex had stopped filing papers and stared absently at the few sheets still on the cabinet top in front of him.

It was a lack of love. A lack of lust. A lack of love and lust for life itself. Or maybe what was lacking was just love. The lack of love had drained everyone of lust for life. Though a lack of lust for life wasn't synonymous with lust for death. Not at all. People lacked the lust for giving themselves fully to life. To be infused with life and happily become undone in it. To live life joyfully. And that wasn't to be confused with all those generic efforts at lust and pleasure that were being undertaken all around him as futile attempts to compensate for the true lust for life itself. Living life sensually was a far cry from being permeated by a lust for life. The way Alex saw it, everyone here had lost that lust for life, and he wasn't even sure how many of them had ever known it or could remember how it felt. There was no lust because the basic feeling that was the fertile soil for it was missing. To feel lust for life, you had to love life itself. And it was this lack of love for life that made their faces

142

wrinkle prematurely, took the shine from their eyes, and smothered the embers in their hearts. They had coffee instead of sleeping in. They bore things instead of experiencing life. Perhaps they also deceived themselves a little. They settled. Tried to fit in. They acquiesced. They accepted that things were as they seemed. They tried to make the best of it. To ignore. To function. That was the happiness of these small-minded people. They were fat and sluggish and stared into emptiness. Unbelievable.

Alex began to sweat. He was all excited. He left the remaining papers on the cabinet, hurried back to his desk, and grabbed the phone. He dialed Jasmin's number. He knew she was working but he had to talk to her. He needed her to talk to him. To remind him why he was here and that staying here was worth it. He wanted to hear her say that he was blind and that's why he couldn't see the light at the end of the tunnel. He needed to believe her.

She did not answer. Alex kept trying. Again and again, he called her number.

Being here felt like being stuck in the middle of a journey. He had stopped in the middle of nowhere and couldn't move on. You only felt stuck if you didn't like where you were. He never liked being here. He'd never liked this job, these people, and certainly not the prospect of spending the rest of his life here. It was back-breaking, mind-numbing. Like dying a little, every single day. All esprit just faded here. If you looked at it this way, this whole place was nothing but a battlefield were people's spirits were beaten into submission and they were transformed into soulless beasts, day after day. Only that there was no blood and no one could or would hear the screams of terror. On the contrary: it was far too cozy and quiet here. Nobody put up a fight.

Alex held on to the telephone. From it came the steady, sonorous, patient tone that told him the line was free. But there wasn't anyone on the other end of it. The tone sounded on and off. Alex listened for a while.

Then he threw the receiver down on his desk and stared absently out the window.

"I need to get out of here," he murmured. "Jasmin, I need to get out of here."

Suddenly there was a hand on his shoulder. Alex turned around. His boss was standing behind him, one hand on Alex's shoulder, a stack of documents under his other arm.

"Good work so far, Al. Efficient and consistently high quality. I like it."

Alex blushed a little and stammered a low "Thanks."

"The other teams are a little behind. I have some documents here that need to be processed and filed. Would it be okay with you if I left them here with you?"

"Sure. No problem."

"Great, didn't expect otherwise. Keep up the good work!" He placed the documents on Alex's desk near the still-beeping receiver and left.

Alex hung up the phone. He took one of the files and started leafing through it. Now they even gave him extra work from other teams because he'd been so fast. It seemed like not everything just dissolved into hollow disinterest. That actually didn't feel too bad. If he got through these files as fast and efficiently as before, they might even give him his own case to work on. He deserved it. And he'd finally learn something new.

No sooner had he finished that thought than he abruptly stopped. With a contemptuous gesture he threw the file back on his desk. It landed on the stack, but its momentum was too great so it slid off the other papers and over the edge and dropped on the floor.

Alex was stunned. He shook his head several times and clicked his tongue irritably. He had almost fallen for it. Almost become one of them. Just give the little doggy a pat on the head, tell him what a good little doggy it was and well done for jumping through the hoop, and voilà: the little doggy wags his tail and jumps again. And the final state of it all was what he saw around him every day, right here in the office. He had to get out of there. If only for the day.

Alex drove home. Since it was early in the day and Jasmin still at work, he walked around the neighborhood for a while. He was far too agitated to stay inside by himself and wait for her. He decided to drink a couple of beers at the bar, but only to settle down again. Several hours later, he was still sitting there. Like most drunks, he swayed to the music on his bar stool, head tilted back, eyes closed. The liquor couldn't obliterate his problems, but it washed them far away enough that they didn't touch him anymore. After a few beers and several shots, the memories of his day felt like a dream from some long ago era while the here and now seemed light and easy. Alex ordered another round and continued his attempts at sway-dancing. One way or the other, sooner or later, it would turn out exactly like this: you got older, the storms quieter, the inner voices would fall silent, your urge would die down, you would sit at the bar and remember the old battles, wounds and pain, and you would laugh at how powerful and intense it had all been. And how useless and destructive too. That especially. In time, even these memories would fade until you knew them to be there somewhere, but couldn't feel them anymore. Just like he couldn't feel them right now. It would all be reduced to images and thoughts. Or not even that – you would only have a faint notion that there once was something different. That you once had felt and lived like that. But nothing would touch you anymore. You would have made your peace with everything. Eternal peace would rule where mighty battles were once raging. It would be like becoming a new person. Or perhaps rather a different person. A person you had longed to be in those dark, cold moments of your youth. Then you would finally arrive at the point that Alex had reached long before. You would know that the only possible happiness in life consisted in downing a few beers and having some lonely little thing suck your dick only to give her what she was craving for the most: a tender kiss and arms to hold her in the night. No more, no less.

Having finished that last thought, Alex downed the rest of his drink. He lost his balance, slipped off his stool, staggered a few steps backwards, and fell. He landed on his butt first before his back and head hit the floor. There was no pain; only a bright flash before his eyes. He smiled and put up one hand to shield his face because he thought it was the sun blinding him. Then he tried to look around and find out where he was. As he turned his head to one side, he saw a woman standing there. He strained to see who it was but she seemed too far away. His feeling told him that she was beautiful. Beautiful and feminine. Glowing with a certainty about life itself. Infused with the wonderful joy and excitement of being human. And anchored down by a touch of honest, true, bitter-sweet melancholy that came from the knowledge that life was only a finite part of infinity. Again he tried to see that woman's face. But the more he tried, the farther she seemed to retreat. Alex wanted to get up and follow her when he suddenly realized where he must be: in the garden of his house by the lake. But there was no house to be seen and the lawn felt hard and cold. He couldn't see the lake, either. What he saw were cranes, earthmovers, and scaffolding. His land had been sold. In the background he heard voices. They were talking to him. It had to be construction workers who wanted him to buzz off. Since he didn't want to move, they grabbed him and carried him off. Alex tried to break free and swore at the men. At last they let go off him and he dropped to the ground. When one of the construction workers asked about a cab, Alex realized that he was lying in the parking lot in front of the bar. Two guys had dragged him out and were about to call him a cab to take him home. Alex picked himself up and waved them off.

Slowly he staggered home, holding on to lampposts and brushing along walls. The exercise – such as it was – and the fresh air sobered him up a little. Enough at least that he could to some extent ponder what to tell Jasmin when he got home. She would be pretty mad, that much was certain. He was about to get lost in his search for possible excuses when he jumped and froze with shock. From an alley entrance directly in front of him sounded the clatter and clang of trashcans that someone must have knocked over.

"Who's there?" Alex shouted, more out of reflex than deliberately.

He took a careful step toward the alley and leaned forward to glance around the corner. That made him lose his balance for the second time that night. He stumbled several clumsy steps forward and ended up right in front of the overturned trashcans. When he got his bearings, he saw the big, burly dog with rumpled fur and gleaming eyes that was growling threateningly at him. Startled, Alex held his breath. Man and beast stared at each other for a long moment. Then the dog sniffed in the trash, picked up something with his teeth, turned around, and trotted down the dark, deserted alley. When the dog was gone, the relief virtually exploded inside Alex. He threw up and fell head long into the heap of trash.

"Damn mutt. Scared me senseless," he swore as he wiped his mouth with his sleeve.

Awkwardly, using the trashcans as support, Alex got up.

"What a dog," he murmured.

And then, shaking his fist in the direction where the dog had disappeared: "Don't let me catch you!"

Slowly, he lowered his fist.

"And where will you sleep tonight, you stupid mutt? All alone under a bridge, on the cold ground?!"

Alex continued to stare into the dark alley.

"What a magnificent dog," he grunted again.

Finally, he turned around and headed home, muttering under his breath:

"Don't let them catch you."

9

Making as little noise as he could possibly manage, Alex snuck into the apartment. Everything was quiet and all the lights were out, so he carefully opened the door to the bedroom. Not primarily to check whether Jasmin was sleeping, but to make sure she was there. The pale light that came through the half-opened door fell on her peaceful face on the pillow, drawing it in fine, smooth contours. For a moment he stood motionless by the bed and watched her sleep. He was glad she was here. Alex knew that she must have been angry when it got later and later and he hadn't come home – hadn't even bothered to call. But still she stayed here. True, it had never been Jasmin's style to just withdraw or even disappear, but the fear that she might be gone still wormed its way deeper and deeper into Alex's mind as he staggered home. The source of this fear was a kind of premonition that had befallen him when he thought about Jasmin and that hadn't led to the familiar feeling of comfort and relaxation. Instead, Jasmin – even the Jasmin of his imagination – seemed slightly strange today, or perhaps rather a little remote. Not as close and intimate as usual. Now, he was relieved that his premonition had been wrong. The soft, steady rise and fall of the blanket over her chest soothed him. He would have liked to get in bed beside her and wrap his arms around her, even though he was well aware that once she woke up, she wouldn't just let him snuggle up to her but demand an explanation. He would not even have minded. Quite the contrary – now that he saw her, he almost yearned to wake and talk to her. Yet she was so beautiful as she lay there sleeping peacefully. He felt closer to her just standing here and watching than if he would actually stretch out his hand and touch her. He often felt this way with Jasmin. Far too often. It was a sensation as if a beautiful, radiant flower was about to unfold in his chest, only to be squashed and buried under a large, heavy rock. This was one of the rare moments were he truly felt his love for Jasmin and hers for him, his happiness of being allowed to be with her, wash through him and take hold of him. And only to realize in the same blink of an eye, that it were moments like this that left him feel suddenly and infinitely lonely. He had never understood why that was. And tonight he was, for sure, too tired and drunk to find an answer. He let Jasmin sleep and lay down on the floor beside the bed.

When he awoke the next morning, he was covered with a blanket. Jasmin had left him fresh orange juice and toast on the table before heading off to work. Alex took a sip of the juice and called in sick at work. Then he went to bed and slept.

It was still afternoon when Jasmin got home that day. She hadn't reached Alex at work so she knew he'd stayed home. That was why she left early – she wanted to check how he was doing. She also had come up with an idea that might cheer him up. She could hardly wait to see Alex's face when she showed him. But when she entered the apartment, the surprise was all hers for the first she saw was empty beer bottles on the couch table and Alex sitting in front of the TV, another bottle in hand. She tried to hide her disappointment and set the box she was holding on the floor. Alex sat up and watched her lift a young dog from the box and carry it over to him in her arms. She stood before him, beaming alternately at him and the dog.

 "Hello, Alexander. Aren't you going to say hello to us?"

"Did you agree to dogsit again?"

"No. This is Buddy. Buddy is our dog."

"You're joking, right?"

"Not at all. Look at him – isn't he just the cutest thing? Come on, stroke his fur."

"The hell I will. And you're blocking my view."

"You're in a fabulous mood again."

"You could have asked before going out and getting a dog."

"But then it wouldn't have been a surprise. Sorry for trying to do something good for you."

"Jasmin, I don't want a dog."

"But I do. And now we have one. Plus, I thought it would cheer you up a little. You're really no fun to be around. Maybe this little guy will bring some joy back into our life."

"I'm sorry. Sorry that I'm not one of the joys in your life and don't even want your dog."

"You are drunk. Again. Is that what you want? Does it make things easier to bear?"

"Yes, I'm drunk. Again. And guess what? It doesn't help. Again. Maybe next time."

"You're impossible. Do you ever consider how it affects me when you behave this way?"

"How exactly do I behave? Or rather, how would you have me behave? Do you want me to wear a collar and hand you the leash so that you can walk me around the block?"

"Go and take a cold shower. You smell and talk nonsense."

"Jasmin, you know I love you and would do anything for you, but you need to talk to me, I-"

"No! You just listen for once!"

Jasmin set the dog down and stood up straight in front of Alex.

"Do you think all this is easy for me?! Do you believe this is the life I've always wanted? I'm doing everything I can to show you how much you mean to me. But you're really not making it any easier. Why do you let things get you down so willingly? And why do you try to pull me down with you? I come home, all excited to introduce you to Buddy, and you just sit there, drunk, and snap at me. What on earth is eating you? You promised me things would be better. Well, you have to make an effort to make this work. You've been telling me how much you admire me for the way I live and love, and how wonderful you think my world must be. I know how much you yearn for it and I would love to show you the way, Alex, but you have to at least try to open up and budge an inch. Guess what? Loving you isn't always easy. You have to allow yourself to be loved. Otherwise, it's all for nothing. And you need to do something for me, too, now and then. It's about giving and taking. I really don't expect all that much, but when you act like this, I don't know what to do with you.

I'm sorry, I truly am, that I can't just fuel you up with life the way your mind dreams and your heart longs to feel. But what do you expect me to do? I can't undo the past and make the future all wonderful. As much as I'd love to do that for you, Alexander. I also have to work at not despairing, being a 'good' person and becoming more, as you like to call it. It's not easy for me to accept and integrate the fact that life isn't always fair. Whether it's to my disadvantage or my advantage. Both. And I have to accept that I have a lot of influence and can work to turn the unfairness to my advantage. But for me, too, there are many factors that are totally out of my control. Especially where other people are concerned. Every day, I have to deal with this and remind myself to believe that every human being will act to his or her best intellectual, spiritual, and emotional capabilities in any given situation and any given moment. Despite the fact that much of what goes on around me indicates that what is often the motive is maliciousness and other grave deficits. I have to struggle to believe in the goodness of humankind. That also involves asking myself again and again whether it's worth the effort. Whether it is right to fight against the inevitable perceived injustices, to defend the rights I believe have been violated, to try and enlighten or even instruct others. To be honest with myself about myself, my strengths, and my weaknesses. About what makes me happy and what destroys my happiness. About what my world, as you call it, is really like: do I try to dream-blur the borders of its reality and distort it? Where do I want it to evolve? And are there corners and regions I do not want to explore or face alone – maybe even can't? This is where I need you, Alexander. I need you to bear this and to continue believing in this world of mine that you love so much – to believe and live and love in it. I need you.

Despite all the adversity and the many cold, dark nights, I want to be able to look back one day and know that I have been the best person I could be and led the best life I could. I want to be able to tell myself that I did everything in my power, everything my character and abilities allowed, to lead a good life. For me, that includes love, first and foremost. I want to have loved, fully and without restraint, giving all that I had to give, regardless of the consequences. This attitude has caused me some disappointments in life, and I have been hurt before. I've been hurt by you, too. As you know, Alexander. But does it look like that's keeping me from moving on? Has it made me withdraw from life and love? I'm still here with you, Alexander. No war has ever kept me from believing in true love. I know that there is such a love, and I want to experience it, Alexander. I want us to fight for it. No matter how few and far between and passing those stolen moments may be in which we slip away into our world of love. No matter what struggles you have to endure out there, how dull and bleak our daily life may sometimes seem to us – I am here for you, Alexander; I am waiting to take you with me to our other world. You just need to follow me.

I have so much hope for us. You're giving me so much hope. Your lips and your eyes tell me honestly and clearly that your whole heart really belongs to me. But where does it keep fleeing with the rest of you? Even when I'm holding you in my arms all night I often feel that I can only hold on to you for a few precious moments. What is it that drives you away? How can I make you truly be here with me? I believe that you love me. But what you love even more is your idea of me. You will never be able to be with me that way. Why else would you rather sleep on the cold, hard ground than with me in the warm, soft bed?

I am here for you, Alexander. And I will do everything I can for you, everything in my power. Why isn't that enough for you? I love you. I love you with all my heart. And all I wish is for you to love me back and spend the rest of your life with me."

Alex sat on the couch and stared at Jasmin. His face showed a mixture of wonder, puzzlement, and horror. Before he could get his thoughts straight, Jasmin broke the silence.

"And with Buddy of course. I want to give you Buddy as a token of my deepest love. Wouldn't that be a wonderful start for our own little family?"

Now Alex rose and walked toward the dining table, beer bottle in hand, taking a big step over the dog that was still sitting on the floor, and snarling: "Get that thing out of here."

Jasmin followed him, took hold of his arm and forced him to stop and face her.

"Alex, please calm down and stop drinking. Start behaving like a grownup."

He set down the bottle on the table and pierced her with his gaze.

"I am very calm. Get it out."

Jasmin shook her head, irritated.

"We'll talk about it tomorrow when you're sober."

She took a few of the empty bottles from the table and headed toward the kitchen. Alex blocked her way.

"I do not want a dog, Jasmin."

"But I do."

As he turned and tried to grab the puppy, Jasmin put the bottles hastily down on the table and threw herself at his back. Some of the bottles toppled over, rolled to the edge of the table, and clattered on the floor. Scared by the noise and the commotion, the dog whimpered and fled into a corner before Alex could pick him up.

He wanted to follow the animal, but Jasmin was on his back now, one arm wrapped around his neck, and pummeled his shoulders and arm with the other hand.

"Alex! Leave the dog alone!"

He grabbed Jasmin's forearms and peeled her off him. When he tried to push her away, she once again hit him on the chest, hard this time.

"Alex, it's not the dog's fault!"

They faced each other, motionless and silent.

Then Alex's hand swooped up and slapped Jasmin in the face.

Frozen, his face a mask of sheer horror, Alex remained standing there for a long time after Jasmin had fled the apartment.

10

"We interrupt this program for breaking news. According to police reports, an armed man entered the First Municipal Bank as it was opening for business this morning and tried to rob it. The police have confirmed that the man was carrying a hunting rifle and holding a small dog. Live from downtown is our special reporter."

The image switched to a reporter holding a microphone. Visible in the background were numerous police cars and an ambulance parked haphazardly on the street. Curious onlookers had gathered behind the police tape. You could not see what was happening beyond, only that more and more policemen pushed through the crowd and disappeared into the sealed-off area. The camera followed the reporter, who moved toward the bank.

"I am standing not far from the bank's main entrance. The police have sealed off a wide perimeter around the building. The exact course of events inside the bank still remains unclear. According to official police statements, the intruder, he himself, instructed the bank personnel to call the police. Afterwards, he seemed to have waited for the law officers to arrive. They have now surrounded him, making any attempt to escape impossible. Inside the bank are five employees and five customers, all of whom seem to be unharmed.

A moment ago, the armed man stepped through the main entrance and is now face to face with a dozen police officers with their weapons drawn. He is negotiating with the commanding officer and has threatened to kill anyone who approaches him without invitation. He has also released the dog and demands that a paramedic gets the animal and takes it to a woman named Jasmin.

The police are still holding back, but this seems like a good opportunity to bring this bank hold-up to an end. The man, who is obviously disturbed, has been ordered repeatedly to give up and turn himself in. However, he is still standing in front of the bank, gun in hand, and making no move towards surrender. Instead he keeps talking incoherently and unintelligibly about someone named "Buddy", who, the man says, "has all this behind him."

Now I see the paramedic approaching the little dog."

The TV image zoomed in on the paramedic, who picked up the dog and retreated to the ambulance. Then you could hear the voice of the officer urging Alex again to surrender. But Alex neither heard nor saw him. In his mind, he was at a lake, lying on the fragrant lawn in front of his house. Slowly he raised the rifle aiming at the nervous policemen. There were several shots. Alex fell dead on the ground.

FSC
www.fsc.org
MIX
Papier | Fördert
gute Waldnutzung
FSC® C083411

Zeitfracht Medien GmbH
Ferdinand-Jühlke-Straße 7
99095 Erfurt, Deutschland
produktsicherheit@kolibri360.de